It was a few minutes to seven, and the light was quickly fading. Few pedestrians were on the streets, and Margaret walked as quickly as her seventy-two-year-old legs would carry her. She stopped for the light on West End Avenue and stepped off the curb. She was still looking up at the light when she felt the pressure of the viselike hands on her waist. She gave a little muffled cry and tried to turn around. But the grip on her waist kept her facing forward.

Forty yards away a panel truck sped to make the light. It would take a simple push at the right moment, and Margaret would become simply another accident statistic. Everything then happened at once. She felt her feet lift off the ground. Then everything went wavy as she hit the pavement with a thud. The last thing she heard above the screech of the van's tires was the sound of running footsteps. . . .

ONE DOLLAR DEATH

Richard Barth

FAWCETT BOOKS • NEW YORK

Library of Congress Catalog Card Number: 82-2555

ISBN 0-449-21813-9

Manufactured in the United States of America

First Ballantine Books Edition: August 1991

FOR
MORGAN NICHOLAS

ONE
DOLLAR
DEATH

One

MARGARET BINTON BIT DOWN ON THE Dixon number two eraserless pencil she was holding and looked up with a frown on her face. Why couldn't she remember? That particular stitch was one of her favorites. She was sure she'd heard it mentioned by one of her friends. She looked down at the crossword again and the definition for number forty-six down: "popcorn stitch." Now, what was it called? She closed her eyes and used an old trick. She placed herself in her Wednesday afternoon knitting group, picturing all of her old friends at the United Order of True Sisters. Then she fabricated a conversation with one about a cable-knit sweater for a grandson, and with another about a jacquard pattern scarf for a young niece. She imagined her friends, knitting needles clicking, chattering away about stitches and particular garments they had made. As she thought, she threaded the pencil idly through her hair. All at once she opened her eyes and smiled.

"Bobble. A bobble stitch. Greta made a vest like that for her husband." She bent over and wrote the word in the empty space. In three minutes the corner of the puzzle was completed and she put her pencil down. "Thirty-eight minutes," she calculated with a sigh, noting the time on her old Timex. "Could be better." She was about to refold the *Times* when she spotted a small notice on the facing page. She read it over once, and her glance traveled immediately to her modest breakfront and an object of abiding ugliness, a pewter teapot

1

with the proportions of a small Victorian coal scuttle. Here at last was an opportunity to rid herself of the horrible thing. Oscar, may he rest in peace, will never know, she thought. And maybe it is worth something. He always claimed it came from a distant relative of the czar. She looked back at the paper and the notice of the Third Annual Sotheby Parke Bernet Heirloom Appraisal Day. "Bring your heirlooms in for appraisal and consignment," the notice read. "Who knows what riches you have in your attic."

It didn't take Margaret long to make up her mind. Forty years, she thought, and not a single decent pot of tea. It's time someone else had the pleasure. In less than three minutes the teapot was in a brown grocery bag, and Margaret was headed across town.

Two

AS SOON AS SHE ENTERED THE AUCTION house, Margaret realized she was in for an unpleasant morning. A milling crowd made it difficult to move, and when she finally got to the tiny elevator she found herself sharing it with the proud owners of a four-foot Chinese vase, a primitive wood-carving the size of a barber's pole, and an ornate brass samovar. Where, she wondered, were the people trying to sell jewelry or small stamp collections? The elevator door gave onto a large foyer with several small rooms opening from it. There were as many people upstairs in the foyer as there were in the downstairs lobby, but now they were grouped together in some loose association. She followed the owner of the samovar as he struggled to a doorway marked RUSSIAN ART. On the way she passed signs for ART DECO, PRE-COLUMBIAN ART, SNUFF BOTTLES, RUGS AND CARPETS, and finally COINS. She was quite exhausted by the time she found a seat in the group of people waiting to see the Russian expert.

She had been there a few minutes wondering whether it was worth all the trouble when she looked up idly at the small group of people nearby waiting to see the coin expert.

"Why, it's Hannah," she said suddenly and waved. But the other woman was turned to the side and didn't see her. Margaret got up with a smile, walked the few feet, and sat down in an empty chair next to her friend.

"Hannah," she said again, and this time the other woman turned around.

"Why, Margaret!" Hannah's face broke out in a broad grin. "What are you doing here?"

"Quite frankly, I don't know," Margaret said pointedly. "All this commotion!" She lit a cigarette, took a puff, and held up the brown bag. "Actually, I thought I'd see about Oscar's aunt's teapot." She opened the bag and pulled it out. "It's supposed to be Russian."

"Lovely," Hannah said.

"Yes, well." Margaret cleared her throat. "I hope they agree." She looked closely at the other woman. Margaret hadn't seen her for two weeks; the last time was at an art lecture at the Florence Bliss Senior Citizen Center. She still had the same friendly smile, neatly combed gray hair, and overrouged cheeks. Margaret liked Hannah Jansen. She was a thoughtful woman who hadn't let her husband Ernest's death five years earlier make her into a recluse like so many others. Each year Margaret received a card from her on her birthday along with a pair of tickets to Radio City Music Hall. Of course Margaret invited her, and they always had fun, although quite frankly she would have preferred a Hitchcock double feature at the Thalia. But seeing her now at the heirloom appraisal was surprising.

"And what," Margaret asked, "are you doing here?"

"Oh, yes," Hannah said. She fumbled in her handbag. After a minute she pulled out a small plastic envelope with a coin in it. Margaret bent closer and saw it was made of silver. It was dated 1804.

"Pretty," Margaret said. "And in good condition. Oscar used to have a few old coins, never amounted to much, but he always told me the most important thing was their condition." She took another puff of her cigarette and crushed it out in a receptacle on a table nearby. She hoped she hadn't used someone's priceless porcelain heirloom as an ashtray. "Where'd you get it?"

"Such a long story," Hannah said, shaking her head. She looked at the coin in her hand with a kind of wistfulness while Margaret waited patiently.

"From Ernest?" Margaret finally prodded after a minute's silence.

"Yes, Ernest," Hannah said slowly and looked up. "He told me he didn't know anything about it. He was just keeping it for Korfstein."

Margaret searched her memory of friends and acquaintances but couldn't place the name. "Korfstein?" she asked finally.

Hannah looked surprised. "The man Ernest worked for in Munich. Didn't I ever mention him to you? Ernest was with him when we married in 1930 and continued up until 1939. A few months before the SS came, Korfstein gave Ernest the coin to keep for him should anything happen. He also gave Ernest some papers, but Ernest could never remember where he put them. After the war Korfstein never showed up. Of course we left a forwarding address in Munich when we came over in forty-eight," she added hastily.

"And Ernest waited patiently for over thirty-five years for Korfstein to reappear?" Margaret asked.

Hannah hesitated for the briefest moment, then looked up into Margaret's eyes. "A short time before he died, he wanted me to sell it. He told me Korfstein was dead. He'd just had a letter from a nephew in Germany who accidentally had bumped into someone Korfstein had befriended at Auschwitz. Korfstein was an old man when he was taken, and apparently he didn't last too long." Hannah shrugged. "By then Ernest was bedridden and couldn't leave the house. He thought the coin might be valuable, and we could use the money for some of the bills. But I couldn't bring myself to sell it. . . . Ernest had protected it for so long." Hannah pulled out a small handkerchief from her sleeve and dabbed at the corner of her nose. "Then before I knew it, he was gone. . . . " The words came slower. "The insurance money came in, so I didn't need to sell the coin at all." There was a pause.

"Until now," Margaret added evenly.

"Oh, Margaret, I'm still not sure what to do," Hannah said in an unsteady voice. "I've no idea what it's worth. I don't even know what it is. Do you think I should sell it?"

Margaret shrugged. "There's no harm in asking advice. Then when you know what it's worth, you can make your decision."

"Yes, that's what I thought, too." Hannah's eyes brightened. "And I needn't sell it if I don't want to."

"Exactly," Margaret reassured her and looked back at the group waiting for the Russian expert. The man with the samovar was just entering his office. "Oh, my," she said hurriedly. "I'd better go or I'll miss my turn. Wait for me, dear, and we'll have a nice cup of tea when this is all over." She patted Hannah's hand and got up and walked back to her corner of the lobby. She was next in line to go in. Three minutes later the man with the brass samovar came out, still struggling with his heavy heirloom. As Margaret waited for him to pass, she glanced quickly in Hannah's direction. She was amused to see her friend talking and showing the coin to another Sotheby customer, a short, elegantly dressed man with red hair. Just like her, she thought, turning back. Always needed a second opinion. She pushed the door open and went in holding the pewter teapot in front of her as though it were as precious as King Tut's unguent jar.

Three and a half minutes later she emerged, the teapot resting securely in the bottom of her bag. Her smile had turned to a frown and she was carelessly muttering to herself. "Forty-five dollars indeed! The nerve of him . . . imitation!" She was so annoyed she didn't look where she was going and barked her shin against the edge of someone's supposedly Russian andirons. Immediately she found herself sitting down to catch her breath.

"That's it, no more." Slowly she got up and took a step toward the door when she remembered Hannah. Her eyes traveled to the coin section, and she was surprised to see her friend still sitting in the same chair. Except now she was all alone. She hobbled over but didn't bother to sit down.

"Hannah, are you finished yet?" she asked brusquely. "This place is a madhouse." She waited for a reply, but Hannah said nothing. She looked closer and saw that her eyes were closed. "Funny," Margaret said as she bent lower. Her friend's hands were crossed politely in front of her, so politely, in fact, that Margaret almost missed the little stain spreading out from underneath them. Then, almost by reflex, Margaret reached out and unbuttoned Hannah's crocheted sweater. Her eyes traced the thin rivulet of blood upward until it ended right over her friend's heart. Margaret screamed, and, even before she thought about it, she knew the coin was gone.

Three

LIEUTENANT EVANS WAS THE NEATEST police detective Margaret had ever seen. Perhaps that was because his beat was the posh silk-stocking district. But the expensive tweed jacket and button-down collar were still unsettling to her. She was used to her friend Lieutenant Morley's rumpled polyester Mays specials and spotted neckties. Besides, Evans didn't smoke, and Margaret as usual had run out of cigarettes. One of the nicest things about Morley was his Camels. She looked back up at the clean-cut detective and frowned.

"I'm afraid I can't help you with that. As far as I know Hannah had no relatives, at least no one here in the United States."

"And friends?"

"Just a handful of us at the center." She took a quick look around the small room that an hour earlier had served as the oceanic-art expert's office. There were still some frightening mud masks on the wall and a beautiful but deadly-looking carved set of bow and arrows in the corner. The setting made her feel even more uncomfortable. Standing next to Evans was another uniformed officer taking things down in shorthand. Margaret turned back to the nonchalant detective. "Lieutenant, I've already told you you're heading in the wrong direction. Hannah was killed for the coin, not by any of her relatives or friends."

"That's as it may be," Evans said airily, "but why don't you let me decide that? Now"—he pulled a stray hair off the lapel of his jacket—"tell me about this center."

By the time Evans got to asking about the coin and their conversation, Margaret was tired and angry. She resented the casual and roundabout questions when she knew that not too far away was a murderer with red hair and Hannah's coin. Finally she couldn't contain herself and said angrily, "Why don't you listen and let me help you? She was my friend."

Evans smiled at her condescendingly. He nodded smugly at the teapot sticking half out of her bag.

"Mrs. Binton," he said slowly, "you may be an expert at brewing tea, but this is murder. I think it's a bit out of your depth."

"Yes, well," Margaret said, turning red. She took a deep breath. "Perhaps you're right. You asked about the coin. . . ." She proceeded to tell them as little as she could about her meeting with Hannah. Insult me, she fumed. In a minute she was finished.

"And that's all?" Evans said evenly.

"Yes, everything. The coin was about this big." She made a circle with her thumb and first finger.

"And the man you saw her talking to had red hair. Could you describe him a little more fully?"

"I only saw him quickly. It was the only impression I had."

"Did you see him or anyone else carrying in a knife for appraisal?" He consulted his notes. "A very thin knife with a diamond-shaped blade."

Margaret shook her head.

"Could you describe the coin, then?" he asked with some vexation. "The date, for instance."

"I don't think I saw the date. . . . But it had the word *Liberty* written on it, and there was a woman with long hair. Does that help?"

The lieutenant was silently studying the eraser on the end of his pencil. "Mrs. Binton, do you know where Mrs. Jansen lived? She didn't have a phone; at least she's not listed."

Margaret hesitated. "Not in my head. They might know at the center."

Evans made a face.

"What's the matter, Lieutenant?"

"Look, Mrs. Binton. I've only got one other man assigned. The least you could do is save us a trip crosstown. You were her friend; you had to know where she lived. Why the act?"

"No act, Lieutenant. I told you the truth. I don't keep addresses in my head. And if you ask me, it's a shame . . . two men! Some East Side coed gets killed and a few dozen men are put on the case. An elderly citizen is murdered, and the best you can do is one assistant. That's not right."

Evans didn't say anything for a long while. Finally he leaned back in his chair.

"Thank you, Mrs. Binton. We'll be in touch." He turned

to the sergeant. "Take her address, Shaughnessy, and send in the next one." He leaned over the desk and waited quietly for her to leave. She didn't need a second invitation. In no time she was back on Madison Avenue and hailing a taxi.

"Two twenty-eight A West One Hundredth Street," she said, carefully replacing her address book in her handbag. "And hurry, please."

Four

HANNAH'S APARTMENT WAS LOCATED IN a building that had few pretensions. The doorman never wore a uniform, the plastic flowers in the lobby were never dusted, and the automatic elevator never started before taking a minute to summon up enough courage for another run. Nonetheless, Margaret remembered the apartment as being a spacious one-bedroom with enough nooks and crannies to make the Collier brothers envious. She nodded politely to the young doorman on watch, who was hunched over a little portable television. She stepped off the elevator on the third floor and went immediately to Hannah's door. She studied it carefully and noticed thankfully that there was enough space around the lock for her senior-citizen transit pass. After a moment of prodding, the lock gave way and Margaret slipped inside. It took her a moment to get over her macabre sensations. Dirty breakfast dishes were still on the kitchen table, and a book lay open by an easy chair. But Margaret had little time for personal feelings. She looked at her watch and saw it was one thirty. She had one hour at best and set to work with remarkable energy.

By two o'clock she satisfied herself the bedroom did not have what she was looking for and came out to the living room. If only there weren't so much junk, she thought, and began looking at all the old papers in the desk drawers. She was careful to put things back in their original places. Several times she heard noises by the front door and held her breath, but fortunately they were just of tenants going to and from other apartments. By two thirty she had assured herself that the desk and the other drawers in the living room held no information about an old coin. She turned around and faced her last possibility, the bookshelf.

Hannah and her husband had been avid readers, and their bookcase took up almost a complete side wall. But Margaret bypassed the hundreds of detective books and *Reader's Digest* condensed books. She was looking for a particular section which she found on the top left shelf. She pulled over a nearby chair and climbed up. Here were perhaps four dozen old clothbound volumes in German and, if Margaret was correct, they had come from Munich with Hannah and Ernest in forty-eight. There were among other things two volumes of poetry by Rilke, a physics textbook printed in 1920, *The Magic Mountain* by Thomas Mann, and collected writings by Hermann Hesse. Margaret took out a book and carefully flipped through the pages. A dry, musty smell caught in her nose, the smell of half-century-old, stale, oxidized paper. The sixth volume she pulled out was a particularly worn Heine from which she noticed a tiny corner of paper sticking up. Slowly she opened the book to the spot and found an envelope. The corner that had been sticking out was yellower than the rest of the envelope, indicating that it hadn't been moved in many years. She removed the envelope, replaced the book, and got down from the chair. The first thing she saw when she opened the envelope was a slip of personal stationery with Otto Korfstein's name engraved on it. She drew it out carefully from the other papers there and was about to read the letter when something else caught her attention. There was another sound coming from the direction of the front door, but this time it didn't go away. And then she distinctly heard a voice she recognized.

"Dammit, which one of these keys do you think it is?" It was Lieutenant Evans.

Margaret didn't even stop to replace the chair. She walked quickly into the bedroom and closed the door. She had remembered correctly; there was a fire escape. The window was an inch open, and Margaret very quietly lifted it the rest of the way, crawled through, and lowered it again. Now what, she wondered. She looked down and saw that the bottom ladder was hiked up to the first floor, and she had no idea how to release it. She started climbing up just as Evans and Shaughnessy found the right key.

It wasn't easy. Margaret had always been afraid of heights, and the building was twelve stories high. She felt her heart pounding by the seventh floor, and she had to stop for breath. At every moment she was afraid either someone would spot her and call the police, or her footsteps on the metal rungs would bring Evans to the window. But neither of those things happened, and she made it to the roof exhausted. Her dress had a long rip where it had caught on a bolt, and her hands were black with soot. She gasped, "Thank God," when the building's roof door opened. One flight down was an elevator landing, and she eagerly pressed the button. In the elevator she pinned the dress back together as best she could with her hatpin and on her way out kept her dirty hands busy looking for something in her handbag. She passed the doorman, still hunched behind his television, without a word. Once outside she turned toward Broadway and didn't look back until she was a block away. The police car was still double-parked in front of the building. No one seemed to be following her. She took a deep breath, found the nearest bench, and sat down.

"Now," she said to herself, "let's see what this is all about." She opened her handbag and pulled out the letter from Korfstein.

Five

ALEXANDER ROSENBLUM LOOKED UP from his crowded desk and saw a pleasant-looking older woman threading her way through the small office. He watched with only mild interest until he realized she was heading toward him.

"Mr. Rosenblum?" she inquired. He nodded. She looked somewhat surprised at the young man in blue jeans and sweat shirt. "I thought you might have been a little older," she confessed. "Your columns sounded so knowledgeable."

He smiled. "I've heard that before. People think if you're under thirty you can't be trusted." He got up, removed a jacket and a stack of books from a nearby chair, and slid it over. She sat down and found a place for her handbag next to a magnifying glass on his desk.

"I hope you don't mind the intrusion," she continued. "My name is Margaret Binton, and I need some advice on coins. From all the magazines I just read at the library, you sounded like you knew what you were talking about." She nodded to the front. "They told me you were in."

"Thank you," Alex said. He leaned back, lifted a sneak-ered foot to the edge of his desk, and looked her over with the bluest eyes she'd ever seen. "What kind of advice?"

"About an 1804 American class two silver dollar."

Alexander Rosenblum laughed for a good ten seconds, a long time considering Margaret didn't understand the joke.

"What's so funny?" she asked, frowning.

"When you came in a minute ago I thought to myself, she collects Susan B. Anthonys or maybe Franklin Mint commemoratives. Hitting me with the 1804 dollar was something of a shock."

"Why is that?"

"Because it's probably one of the three most valuable coins in the world after the Brasher doubloon and the silver decadrachm. The last one went for four hundred thousand in 1980."

"There's only one?" Margaret asked.

"Fifteen, although in fact as I recall there's only one class two and that's at the mint."

She looked puzzled. "How does it differ from the others?"

"The class ones and threes?" He shrugged. "The twos weren't lettered around the edge, the others were. Also the class ones were minted in 1834 or –35 and the twos and threes were minted in 1858."

Margaret held up her hand. "Wait a minute. I thought we were talking about the 1804 dollar."

"We are," Alex said. "The U.S. Mint did some pretty flaky things in the middle of the nineteenth century. The fact is there was no silver dollar coinage between 1804 and 1836, only fractional coinage." Margaret looked blank. "You know, halves and quarters."

"Oh." She nodded.

"Too many of the dollars were leaving the country for use in trade abroad. But in 1834, proof sets of U.S. coins were needed for diplomatic gifts, and for some strange reason the mint employees struck off the 1804 dollar. No one knows how many, but only eight remain."

"Then why the 1858 minting?"

Alex smiled. "Deliberate malfeasance. The director of the mint, a guy by the name of Dubois, needed rare coins to trade with collectors for the mint's own coin collection. The 1804 was a rarity by then, so Dubois just had some extra ones minted. They still had the old dies." Alex chuckled.

"Except they used a slightly different reverse, almost unnoticeable, but that's what separates the two mintings."

"And the class two was minted in 1858 also?" Margaret looked confused.

"Yes, but not for Dubois. That's the strangest story of all. It seems an employee at the mint, no one knows who, had access to the dies and decided to turn a quick buck. He made five 1804 dollars, stupidly not lettering the edge, and tried selling them some ten years later. But he didn't get very far. As soon as they were offered, there was a great hue and cry from the people who owned the originals. Four of the five were returned to the mint. They kept one for their collection and destroyed the other three."

"And what about the fifth one, the one that wasn't returned?"

"Has never been seen." There was silence for a minute while Margaret digested this information.

"Do you think it's possible it still exists?" she said finally.

"Possible, but highly improbable. It would have to have been buried somewhere for the past seventy-five years to have escaped notice. The financial temptation on the owner would be incredible. Today that coin would be worth a fortune."

"Mr. Rosenblum," she continued. "Let's just say for the sake of argument I had that coin." She hesitated. "Who would want it, I mean to the extent they'd do anything to get it?"

"If it were the real class two, minted in 1858, only about a hundred collectors who'd have enough money to buy it and maybe ten thousand who'd steal, bribe, and sell their mothers into slavery to get it. You're talking about something that makes a mint 1923 Bugatti small potatoes. But if you ask me"—he winked at her—"I'd say your 1804 class two was a counterfeit. They're common as three-penny nails. Back in the thirties I think some banks were using them as a promotion stunt. Every week another 1804 turns up at a dealer somewhere without a bona fide provenance, and invariably they turn out to be fakes."

"Provenance?"

"Yeah, authentication . . . you know, a pedigree. Most of them come in with a crazy story attached, like they were found at the bottom of an old drainpipe."

"I see." Margaret lit a cigarette and tossed the match into a nearby wastebasket. "You mean to say that's the only way to tell if a coin is authentic?"

Alex laughed. "Hardly. Let's say it's like a sign of good faith, and of course it legitimizes the ownership. No serious collector ever has a valuable coin without a provenance, but there are ways to tell a genuine coin from a fake."

"With the 1804?"

"Especially with the 1804."

Margaret leaned back and took a puff on the cigarette. "How?"

Alex seemed to be enjoying this. He pulled up his other sneakered foot onto the desk and fixed his gaze for a moment on the ceiling. Margaret waited patiently.

"I'll give you three ways," he said finally. "There are several others, but these are the easiest. First, there's no vertical serif at the end of the horizontal bar on the four in the date. There is, however, a base. Second, where the base intersects with the upright on the four, it intersects at right angles; there is no fillet."

"No what?"

"Fillet." Alex made an arc with his hand. "You know, a curve." He let that sink in. "And third, and this is only on the class two and three, the obverse and reverse juxtaposition is abnormal by about five degrees."

"Whew. And those are the easiest." Margaret crushed out her cigarette and shook her head. "You really are an expert. Tell me, Alexander, how many people do you think could have told me that?" She looked straight at him. "I mean without looking it up."

He smiled. "The 1804 dollar happens to be a favorite of mine." He shrugged. "I suppose there are maybe a dozen other people in the country who know that offhand."

"And in New York?"

"In New York?" He sat upright and turned his blue eyes on Margaret. "No more than five."

"Last question," Margaret said, "then I'll leave you to your coins. Who are they?"

Alex picked up a pen, wrote out several names, and passed the paper across the desk. "I won't even ask why," he said with a smile.

"Good, then I needn't avoid answering." She returned the smile. "Thank you, you've been most helpful." She got up and walked back out of the magazine office. His eyes followed her until she'd closed the door behind her.

Six

IT WAS NOT QUITE BY ACCIDENT THAT Margaret bumped into her friend Bertie later that afternoon. Bertie as usual was parked on their favorite bench on Broadway and Eighty-second Street. A small army of pigeons was pecking around her feet for the handful of crumbs she had just thrown onto the pavement. It was the last handful of the afternoon, and Bertie carefully folded and tucked the brown bag into one of the pockets of her very serviceable but worn raincoat. When she looked up, Margaret was beside her.

" 'Lo," Bertie said happily and leaned to kiss her on the cheek. As she did, Margaret caught the pleasant odor of lavender, Bertie's favorite.

"Afternoon, Bertie," she answered. "I think your followers are growing in numbers," she said, motioning toward the birds.

"You think so?" Bertie sounded pleased.

"Spiking the bread crumbs again?"

Bertie blushed. "Well, just an extra little bit of caraway seed thrown in . . . it's only for the protein. The winter was tough on 'em."

Margaret laughed. "Next thing you'll be cooking them waffles."

"Oh, go on." Bertie gestured with her hand. "What else I got to do anyway?" She leaned forward and made some cooing noises at the nearest birds. Margaret shrugged, unfolded a newspaper she had just purchased, and sat back. The two women did not speak for a few moments. Finally Margaret said, "You hear about Hannah?"

Bertie nodded and straightened up. "I wasn't going to mention it. You were much closer to her than I was."

"It's a shame," Margaret said. "And I was right there when it happened."

"You were!" Bertie said in a voice loud enough to scare the nearest pigeons into flapping their wings.

"I mean I wasn't there when she was killed, mind you. We only chatted a few minutes beforehand." Margaret leaned a little closer and lowered her voice. "But I think I saw someone suspicious just as I was going in to get an appraisal on Oscar's teapot."

"No!" Bertie gasped, and this time the nearest pigeons actually flew away. "Who?"

"I don't know." Margaret opened her purse. "But I think I can find out. The trouble is—" She hesitated. "I need some help." She looked straight at her friend.

Bertie's eyes narrowed. "If this is another one of your detective games—the last time you had me stealing through the night with shovels and all."

Margaret chuckled. "No, no shovels this time." She reached into the open bag. "Just an old, valueless coin and an innocent story. I need to find out what five men look like."

Bertie was silent for a minute, staring at the coin in Margaret's hand. "Where'd you get that?" she finally managed.

"Just one of the old coins Oscar kept. Can't be worth more than a few dollars, but it will be an adequate cover. You see"—she pulled out the list Alex had given her—"I think one of these men did it. They're all coin dealers and run legitimate businesses. All I want you to do is go in to each one, ask the owner to give you an appraisal, and then tell me what he looks like. It's really quite simple, no risk at all."

"I knew it!" Bertie's eyes fluttered closed, then shot open again. "You're asking me to talk to a murderer." She took a deep breath. "What's he look like?"

Margaret shook her head. "If I told you beforehand, you'd be so nervous you'd ruin everything. You could never keep a straight face. That's why I always beat you in canasta."

"But, Margaret . . ." Bertie started, but couldn't find anything else to say. She looked at the coin, and in the silence that followed Margaret knew she'd just recruited an assistant.

"Why can't you do it?" Bertie finally asked, but the question was halfhearted.

"Because I don't want him to see me just yet. I'll tell you all my plans afterward, Bertie, but first you have to do this little job. Here's the list and the coin. We'll meet tomorrow at five sharp. Any questions?"

"Just one," Bertie said, rising. "Your friend Morley in on this one?"

"Not yet. So far we're on our own."

Seven

BERTIE'S "LITTLE JOB" WAS NOT AS EASY AS
Margaret had made it sound. The first name on her list had
moved his office, and it took Bertie most of an hour and a
half to track down the new one. By the time she got to the
second person on the list, he was out to lunch. Bertie decided
to wait and lost another hour. The third dealer was in a meeting downtown and Bertie, having learned her lesson, decided
not to wait and went on to the next name. He refused to see
her when she stated her business on the intercom, saying he
no longer did appraisals off the street. Bertie thought fast and
told him she had been referred by the museum.

"Which one?" the intercom barked.

"One on Eighty-second Street," she answered. After a
deadly long ten seconds she heard the buzzer click open the
door.

After that she went back to the previous dealer, who was
now in and who provided her with a sarcastic and very quick
consultation when she unveiled Oscar's 1910 British halfpenny.

"It was as common," she was told, "as fish and chips in
Liverpool."

Her final expert lived on the Upper West Side. He was
both accessible and cordial and spent several minutes telling
Bertie about the history of the British halfpenny. Had it not
been for him, she would have been cross with Margaret for
a week. As it was, when she saw her friend at five that after-

19

noon, she was, if not brimming over with excitement, certainly pleased with herself.

"I saw them all," she said even before sitting down. "Just like you asked."

"And?"

"I think it's the Russian on Fifty-third Street. He was the most unpleasant."

"Bertie," Margaret began patiently. "I'd rather just have the descriptions."

"Even insultin'. Told me I had no business wasting his time."

"Bertie!"

"Okay." Bertie snorted. "Thought you'd like to know my views." She sat back on the bench, rocked herself a little sideways until she felt more comfortable, and began talking. She gave Margaret full descriptions of the men. Every now and then she digressed into additional opinions, and Margaret had to bring her back to the facts she was so eager to hear. When Bertie was finished, she took out her handkerchief, blew her nose, and waited for Margaret to speak. It was a sign of her anticipation that she didn't even notice the four pigeons staring at her expectantly three feet away. Margaret's eyes were closed, trying better to picture the men she'd heard described. After a minute she looked up, and a little smile crossed her face. "From what you've said, Bertie, I think it's Mr. Zarchin."

"It can't be," Bertie said with shock in her voice. "He was the nicest one."

"That's right, but the only one with red hair. And what you regarded as 'nicely done up' I registered as elegance. Now that I think back, he was wearing a gold collar bar like you said. No, I think he's our man. His friendly personality was probably what persuaded Hannah to show him the coin in the first place. Besides, the others are out. Your choice, the Russian, is bald, and the rest don't fit the description either."

"I'm never wrong," Bertie said with finality. She folded her hands in front of her and looked the picture of disbelief.

"Of course you've been wrong," Margaret said with a chuckle. "Who was it thought Denise Darcel was going to be the biggest star of the sixties?"

"That was different." Bertie blushed.

"It doesn't matter," Margaret continued. "I plan to prove it anyway."

"How?"

Margaret hesitated. "First I'm going to meet him and get him to show me where the coin is. Then I'm going to have Morley arrest him with it."

"Fat chance of that if he's the one," Bertie said.

"Oh, no, he'll do it," Margaret insisted, "because he won't suspect I'm anything other than the wealthy, harmless old widowed coin collector I'm going to pass myself off as." She smiled. "I'll play to his pride."

This time it was Bertie's turn to laugh. "But, Margaret, you don't know a thing about coins. And he's an expert."

"Oh, tosh, that's what libraries are for. I'm not worried about that," Margaret said, patting her friend's hand. "Hardest thing is convincing Morley I haven't lost all my marbles."

"Well," Bertie said, "maybe you should try first with me."

Eight

LIEUTENANT MORLEY LOOKED UP FROM his desk with a scowl on his face. Sorting through the new regulations on the correct distribution and wearing of bulletproof vests was hard enough without the constant interruptions. He stabbed his cigarette out in the sea of butts in the ashtray, took a swallow of cold coffee, and growled, "Yeah!" It sounded like an A train rumbling to a stop.

The door swung open, and Sergeant Shaeffer stuck his head through up to the little gold earring. His face still had a fresh look to it even under the beard. It was only when the rest of him was visible, the torn jeans, the old Adidas, and the stained University of Honolulu sweatshirt, that one got the impression he was not debutante-escort material. Not that his attire as undercover cop for the Eighty-first Precinct was anything other than normal for him . . . even the earring was as much a part of David Shaeffer as his sarcastic grins.

"Someone to see you, boss. An old friend."

"No time for friends now," Morley said. He pulled the paper he was reading closer.

"Oh, yes, you do," Margaret said as she brushed past Shaeffer into the office. "Imagine, after all the cookies I've baked for you." She shook her head.

"He didn't say it was you, Margaret." Morley got up with a smile. "Because if he had I would have locked the door." He held out his hand.

"Go on, they can't be that bad. Last batch went over very well at the center's bazaar." She sat down in her favorite chair by Morley's desk, the one near his pack of Camels. "And here's the new batch. My special." She beamed at him, handing over a small box. "Maple pistachio lace cookies." As she sat back, she snatched out one of his cigarettes.

Morley frowned and looked at her closely. "I don't like it, Margaret. Last time you made lace cookies you wanted me to close down a movie theater."

"A porno den of the worst kind." She bristled. "They should have stayed with the old movies, much better." She lit the cigarette casually.

"But a legitimate business nonetheless," Morley said. "Nothing we could do." He leaned back. "What's on your mind this time?" He grinned up at Shaeffer, who was now focusing on the box of cookies. "You want Dave to investigate a case of a missing shopping cart?"

"Lieutenant, I don't like it when you're patronizing. It doesn't suit you at all." She inhaled on the cigarette and carelessly blew smoke in Morley's direction. "No, I'm afraid it's a case of murder."

"Again." Shaeffer sat down and turned his attention on her. "Are you sure?"

"Of course I'm sure. Your friends across the park at the Nineteenth Precinct are handling it, although they refuse to take my help. Bungling it, if you ask me."

"Who got killed?" Morley asked, opening the box and taking out one of the cookies.

"Hannah Jansen."

Morley looked to Shaeffer for assistance. "Old woman killed at Parke Bernet," Shaeffer said. "Typical splashy East Side murder." He scratched his beard. "Widowed, motive unclear, weapon missing but something like a stiletto . . . made a very thin diamond-shaped wound. That's all I remember."

"Ha!" Margaret said. "Motive as clear as day."

Morley turned to Margaret. "Why us?"

"Because Hannah lived in your precinct." She hesitated. "And so does the murderer." There was silence for a minute. Finally Morley reached out for his second cookie.

"You want to tell us about it?"

"That's why I'm here," she said, and crushed out the cigarette. She leaned back in the chair and began her story. In fifteen minutes she had run through the whole thing: her conversation with Hannah, the finding of the envelope, her talk with Alex, and Bertie's role. When she was finished, she pulled out a yellowed piece of paper and handed it across the desk. "And here's the provenance," she concluded, "in perfect order."

Morley and Shaeffer bent closer to look.

"It's got a notarized signature from the dealer whom Korfstein purchased the coin from in 1895 and also a full description." Margaret produced another piece of paper. "Here is the letter from Korfstein signing the coin over to Ernest Jansen for safekeeping. It's all there.'' She reached for one of her cookies and ate it slowly while the two men inspected the documents. Morley was the first to speak.

''You should give these to the officer in charge at the Nineteenth Precinct.''

''Lieutenant Evans! Are you kidding?'' she said. ''That's like giving a digital watch to a chimpanzee. Besides, this case takes special handling.'' She looked at Shaeffer. ''I'm sure this Mr. Zarchin is no fool. He's hidden that coin by now where an army of cops couldn't find it, and Evans doesn't even have that. No, we need the light touch, if you know what I mean.'' She crunched down on the last bite of lace cookie.

''You mean, Morley corrected, ''your light touch.''

''Exactly.''

Shaeffer rolled his eyes to the ceiling. Morley lit his own cigarette.

''Here's how I figure it,'' Margaret continued. ''We've got the provenance proving the coin belonged to Hannah; we've got the acknowledged fact that only two of these coins exist and one is at the U.S. Mint; we've got or will have my sworn testimony I saw Hannah with the coin in her possession minutes before the murder, and that I saw Zarchin talking to her just before she was found dead. It seems to me all we need is to find the coin in his possession, and we have an ironclad case against him.'' She looked around. ''Am I right?''

The two policemen looked at each other.

''Possibly,'' Morley said.

Shaeffer stood up and walked to the window. He looked down the two stories into the street and at the several people passing by. ''But, Margaret,'' he said, turning around, ''even you think he's hidden the coin already, and the whole thing depends on catching him with it. It could be anywhere . . . a safe deposit box, buried upstate, under his floor.''

''Could even be out of the country,'' Morley added.

''It could,'' she said, ''but that's what I plan to find out.''

''How?'' Morley said with some annoyance.

"Leave that to me. I'm just here to make a deal with you. After I find the coin, you get all your legal warrants and whatnot and then arrest him." She paused for a breath. "Is that a deal?"

Morley crushed out his cigarette after only two puffs.

"I don't like your putting yourself in danger without our even knowing what you're doing."

"What I plan to do is perfectly safe, I promise. Besides, you couldn't stop me if you wanted. All I need to know is you'll be behind me when I tell you where the coin is. If you turn me down, the only thing left is a citizen's arrest, and you know how flimsy they are."

"That sounds like a threat!" Morley shook his head.

"No, only a polite request." She smiled at both of them.

Shaeffer came over. "How will you know it's the right coin?"

Margaret tapped a shopping bag which had gone unnoticed at her feet. "I've got eight books on coins in there and another eight at home. I'll know. And don't forget, I've already seen it."

After a moment Shaeffer raised a hand in indecision.

"What about it, Sam? How bad could it be? Margaret finds the coin, and we bust him. He's in our precinct."

"I've got a choice?" Morley said sarcastically. He glared at Margaret. "If I didn't know you so well, I'd just laugh it off. But"—he shrugged—"every now and then you're lucky. So, okay, I'll go along. Only, if you get in any hot water, you let us know . . . pronto." He leaned back. "What's the guy's name?"

"Frenos Zarchin." She got up, lifted the bag of books, and headed to the door. "I knew you'd be reasonable. That's just what I told Bertie." In a second she was gone.

The two policemen looked at each other in silence.

"Now, why did I do that?" Morley finally asked.

Shaeffer shrugged. "Best maple pistachio cookies east of the Hudson?"

"Ha!" Morley answered. "This time she burned them."

Nine

TWO WEEKS AFTER MARGARET'S MEETING with Morley, old Pancher Reese called an ad hoc meeting of the four people sunning themselves on the Eighty-second Street benches. It was unusual for Margaret to disappear for several days; two weeks without a trace of her was cause for serious worry. It was one forty-five P.M., and Roosa was working on his usual afternoon pint bottle of Thunderbird. He wiped his moist lips with a crumpled handkerchief, recapped the bottle, and looked up at Pancher.

"I dunno," maybe she's sick." His voice had the clarity of a Jersey swamp.

"Never." Pancher's hands fidgeted with the quick nervous movements of a retired OTB clerk, his gray cap bouncing back and forth like a string of two-dollar bets. "She's never been sick a day in her life. And she always tells us when she's going to her nephew's." He frowned and the lines in his face shifted a few degrees off the perpendicular. "She speak to you, Rena? . . . Rena?"

Rena Bernstein rotated the volume dial on the little transistor and pulled the plug out of her ear. A mangy black Persian lamb jacket was draped loosely around her even though it was a warm afternoon. It would probably be draped around her through late June since she loved showing off a good purchase. This one had been twenty-eight dollars at the Masonic Thrift Shop.

". . . Rena?"

"What, Pancher!" She tried to look cross, but instead it came across like a twinge of heartburn. "Right in the middle of *Turandot*."

"The hell with your soap operas. Where's Margaret?"

"Margaret?" Rena looked blank. "Haven't seen her for two weeks. Ask Bertie."

"Bertie is not here yet," Joe Durso said coolly from the end of the bench. "And will not be here until after lunch when she picks up the leftover bread from Pacarelli's." He put his old chipped pipe to his mouth and held a match to its end. As a retired schoolteacher Durso was their resident intellectual and had his image to protect.

"We thought she confided in you," he continued. "There's always some conspiracy with you women."

Rena shook her head. "Maybe Sid," she said casually and replaced the plug in her ear. Her hand went back to her pocket, and they could hear faint strains of music again.

"I hear someone mention my name?" The three others looked up and saw Sid hovering over them. The *Daily Racing Form* was sticking out of the pocket of his plaid jacket where he always kept it, and his sunglasses were shading his eyes. A half-smoked cigar stuck out from under his neatly trimmed white mustache.

"We were wondering about Margaret," Pancher said. "None of us has seen her."

Sid walked slowly around the bench and sat next to Rena. More than anyone else in their group he looked like he'd seen a little luxury in his life—an Arthur Fiedler on the skids. He ran a knuckle down the length of his nose, sucked on the unlit cigar for a moment, and coughed once.

"I just came from there," he said with the satisfaction of someone who can't wait to have a secret dragged from him. "She sends all of you her regards. Says she'll be tied up for a while and not to worry." He leaned back on the bench and leisurely lit his cigar. "Nice day today, ain't it, Rena?"

"Sidney," Durso said, his face turning red. "We haven't all day to play this ridiculous cat-and-mouse. What is taking place?"

Sid raised an eyebrow. "Taking place? I don't know what you mean."

Roosa burped. "I think he wants a fat lip." He started to get up.

"Okay, okay." Sid puffed up five seconds of dense, rancid cigar smoke and looked around. "She's studying about coins, just like she was in college or something. She's got dozens of books all over the place, pictures, magazines, newspapers. You name it. Everywhere you look in that damn apartment there's something else."

"Coins?" Durso said slowly.

"Yeah, little round things."

There was silence for a minute.

"Why?" Rena asked, surprising everyone. Then they saw the plug was disconnected from the radio. "She was never interested in coins before."

"Don't ask me." Sid shrugged. "She didn't say much, just something about it having to do with Hannah's murder."

"Not like her," Roosa said thickly, "trying to cash in on the death of a friend." He took another swallow of the Thunderbird wine and let the bottle slide back down to the bottom of the brown bag.

"No," Sid said. "She's trying to help solve it." He pulled at the cigar again, but it was out.

"Then why did she ask you over?" Durso asked with a note of envy in his voice. "I didn't know you were a numismatist."

Sid stamped the stogie out under his foot and laughed.

"No, and I ain't a numitast, whatever that is. She asked me over because she thought I could help." He hesitated, looking ruefully at the dead cigar, then up at the four others. "She thought I could get my hands on something she needed."

"What?" Pancher asked.

"A chauffeur's outfit."

"A chauffeur's outfit," Rena said. "What on earth for?"

"I don't know, but she said she wanted me in it."

Ten

THE FOLLOWING WEDNESDAY MARGARET walked into Parke Bernet as though she were its majority stockholder. The auction house had returned to the staid, quiet establishment of renown. The downstairs receptionist was immediately accessible and in a polite, clipped British accent told Margaret that the ancient and modern coin auction would be taking place in fifteen minutes on the sixth floor. She gave the man following Margaret only a cursory glance since chauffeurs were a common sight at Parke Bernet, especially ones escorting well-off older women. Once in the elevator Margaret straightened Sid's cap and gave him some last-minute instructions.

"Just remember," she said, smiling, "try and be respectful."

"I feel stupid," he said, pulling at his tight collar. "And I'm dying for a cigarette."

"So am I." The elevator opened and Margaret swept out. She was wearing her most expensive suit, a trim navy-blue worsted that she highlighted with her favorite piece of jewelry, the single strand of pearls Oscar had given her on her sixty-fifth birthday. Her visit to the beauty parlor the day before had added a final touch. Her hair was now neatly coiffed into a tight bun. Followed by Sid in his gray chauffeur's uniform, she was quite the picture of old-world money. She stopped at the desk, purchased a catalogue, and then followed the signs for the auction.

The first thing she noticed upon entering the large carpeted room was what appeared to be a small wooden pulpit off to the right. Above this was a strange contraption which reminded her of the departure notice board at Grand Central Station, except that where train times would have been, pound, mark, franc, and yen quotes were displayed. Directly in front and to the left of the pulpit was a stage, and in the center of the stage was a screen.

"Where to?" Sid whispered.

Margaret jumped nervously. "Shhh. Let me look."

For the first time her glance traveled to the crowd. She was surprised to see that most of the people were men in their forties and fifties, and many were without ties. Out of the hundred or so people there, she was one of the only women. Still, after a half minute she saw the man she was looking for. Actually she spotted the red hair first, then the gold collar bar, and when he turned fully around she recognized him positively as the same man who'd been talking with Hannah.

"Follow me," she said without turning, and headed toward the front.

The auction was just beginning as Margaret found two empty seats a row in front and a few places to the side of the man with red hair. She opened the catalogue on her lap and sat back to wait.

A woman climbed into the pulpit, welcomed everyone, and introduced herself. Four men in beige coats fanned out on either side of the stage and faced the audience with intense and searching eyes. A coin flashed on the screen, the auctioneer called out, "Lot number one, Augustus the Third ducat dated 1734 . . . with a floor at three hundred fifty. Do I hear four hundred?" and the auction began. In twenty-five seconds the coin was knocked down at two thousand, and another coin flashed on the screen. Immediately one of the men in beige trotted up the aisle to a man on Margaret's right, asked him to sign a form, then returned to his watching-post up front.

"They don't kid around," Sid whispered, but it was lost

in the smack of the gavel as the auctioneer quickly disposed of the second coin.

For all Margaret had heard about expensive auctions, there was very little earlobe pulling or newspaper tapping going on. Bidders made no attempt at masking bids and everyone went about the business of transferring the two hundred lots with great efficiency. After a while Margaret's attention drifted. The coins were pretty to look at on the screen, and the 1806 Maximilian One Joseph thaler even looked like an Alfred Hitchcock commemorative, but they went with such speed it was hard to stay fully alert. Then the 1852 1 Augustus Humbert twenty-dollar gold proof came up, and there was a noticeable shift in the mood. A rash of coughing broke out, papers shuffled, and voices were lowered. It was almost as though a hundred collective breaths were taken, and at once the room settled down to wait. The estimate for the coin, not including the ten percent additional buyer's premium, ran to two hundred thousand. It was the queen of the day's auction.

Margaret was dying for a cigarette, but there were several signs prohibiting it. On three occasions the men in beige had enforced the rule with people nearby. She closed her catalogue and moved a little forward in her seat. Out of the corner of her eye she saw the man with red hair pull out a pen for the first time all afternoon. Then, in the electric silence, the auctioneer began. The bidding went very quickly up to one hundred thousand with six bidders competing. At one hundred twenty thousand and again at one hundred sixty thousand several bidders dropped out. The auctioneer looked in her direction, and Margaret watched as her neighbor's pen signified the next bid.

"Thank you, one seventy. Do I hear one eighty?"

Margaret just spotted the tall man in the yellow sweater farther up front as he nodded his head.

"One eighty against you in the back. Do I hear one ninety?" The pen rose and the auctioneer looked down front again.

"I have one ninety, at two we must go in increments of twenty."

The nod came, but it was somewhat slower. The man to Margaret's left flashed his pen almost at the same time the auctioneer looked back in his direction. One of the men in beige relayed the bid: "Two twenty."

"It's now two forty, two forty." She waited. "Do I have two forty?" The man in yellow signified "no" with the tiniest dispirited turn of his head. "Two forty," she intoned once more, canvassing the room with a sweep of her eyes. "Fair warning. Any advance on two twenty?" As she said this she picked up the gavel. At the same time Margaret raised her hand high over her head.

"Yes!" two of the men in beige shouted out simultaneously. "Two forty." The room stirred. The auctioneer said with delight, "We have a new bidder."

Margaret turned to her left and watched the man with the gold collar bar and red hair. As casually as if he were plucking a cherry, his hand rose and the pen with it.

"Two sixty."

"Two eighty," the men in front announced as they saw Margaret's hand rise without the least hesitation.

"Looking for three," the auctioneer said. "It's against you, sir." All the eyes in the room now turned in the direction of the other bidder. Margaret felt a viselike grip on her arm.

"What are you doing?" Sid whispered vehemently. He was almost as ashen as his uniform. "You know what you've done, you've just bid two hundred and eighty thousand dollars for a little piece of metal. Are you crazy? How much you got in your savings account?"

Margaret leaned ever so slightly toward him.

"One hundred and twenty-nine dollars, Sidney, but please mind your manners. Chauffeurs should be seen and not heard. I know what I'm doing." She straightened up and smiled in the direction of the man with red hair just as he raised his pen. He returned the smile, but behind it was a look of curiosity.

"Three hundred thousand," the auctioneer said. The display above the pulpit chattered as it translated the bid into the four other currencies. In the silence it sounded like a gathering of magpies.

"Phew," Sid breathed and released his grip. "Thank God." He wiped the perspiration away from under his eyes. Margaret paused for a second, faced forward, and raised her hand. This time, however, she only brought it to eye level.

"Three hundred and twenty thousand dollars. Thank you, madam. To you, sir, at three forty."

Margaret turned slightly to her left and felt her insides go soft. The other bidder had replaced the pen in his pocket and was slowly shaking his head.

"Three forty, do I hear three forty?" The auctioneer was looking directly at him but getting no response. "Your bid, madam, at three twenty. Any advance on that?" Again her eyes scanned the entire room in case there was a new bidder, but her gaze came back to rest on Margaret as she picked up the cylinder-shaped gavel. "Fair warning!" She hesitated for three seconds and slowly raised the piece of wood. Margaret saw her lips purse into the beginning of "sold" when she heard the yell "Three forty" from up front. One of the men in beige was pointing excitedly to Margaret's left. The man with red hair had decided to bid without his pen.

Margaret stood up slowly, motioned for Sid to follow, and walked to the back of the room. She tried to walk as steadily as possible, but under the circumstances it took great effort. By the time she arrived at the door, the coin had been hammered down at three hundred and forty thousand dollars to the man with the red hair. Margaret paused just briefly and, in the ensuing applause, Sid opened the door for her. Then she walked through into the empty foyer and smiled.

"I told you I knew what I was doing." She took a deep breath. "Now we wait, right here by the elevator."

It didn't take long. Within a minute the door opened again, and the man with red hair walked through. Without hesitation he came up to her and held out his hand.

"Please, I'd like to introduce myself," he said. "I'm Frenos Zarchin. Might I know who you are?" He gave her a wry smile. "I think I have that privilege inasmuch as you've just cost me one hundred and twenty thousand dollars."

"And you just cost me the coin, Mr. Zarchin," Margaret replied evenly. "But fair's fair." She shrugged. "I'm Mrs. Cornelius Sloan." She took his hand and shook it. "Congratulations."

"Sloan?" Zarchin knitted his forehead. "I don't recall a Sloan in the field."

"Oh, I know, Mr. Zarchin, but you will. I'm just getting started." She smiled. "Ever since my husband died, that is. Poor man, never understood the value of coins. Had all his money tied up in scrap metal. Imagine that . . . such hideous stuff. Isn't that right, Sidney?"

"Yes, ma'am," Sid replied with the greatest respect.

Zarchin looked at him, then back at her closely.

"The Humbert's quite a big play to start off with."

"Oh, I'm not really just starting, Mr. Zarchin. Let's say I'm just starting to specialize. I played around with Greek coinage including the drachms and those silly staters and obols until they were coming out of my ears. Far too many being dug up to suit me. What's rare one day can be worthless the next if some archeology student gets lucky. No, I decided to stick with true rarities, where your investment is safe. That's when I started purchasing the Colonial coins like the Pine Tree shillings." She lowered her voice. "You know, I even have a good 1739 Higley copper."

Zarchin raised an eyebrow. "Where'd you get that?"

"Privately, Mr. Zarchin, privately. And I can assure you it was much harder to get than my Newby farthing. Did you know," she continued, "it's my favorite, I mean the Newby. It has such a funny little motto—*Quiescat Plebs*."

Zarchin smirked. "Yes, I know. 'May the people be quiet.' I happen to have one, too."

"Indeed," Margaret laughed. "So you see, that's how I came to American coinage and the Humberts. But then, Mr. Zarchin, you bought my coin away from me. That was naughty. Although I must admit to lose out to you was something of an honor. You have such a reputation. . . ."

Zarchin smiled. "I don't know. . . ."

"One of the best collections in the East. One of the three 1822 Half Eagles, I understand."

He nodded with a modest elegance.

"I've never seen one," she said without a trace of self-consciousness. "Are they as pretty as the books make out?"

"Quite." He hesitated. Margaret could tell he was trying to decide something. "Would you like to see it?"

"The 1822? I'd love to."

Zarchin reached into a pocket of his jacket and produced a card. "My office," he said. "Please call anytime, and I'll arrange to show you some of the collection."

"Oh, how delightful you are, Mr. Zarchin. I shall certainly do that." Margaret shook his hand again. "And now I really must leave," she added. "I'm afraid I'm late." She turned to Sid, who had been waiting attentively at the elevator. "Shall we go, Sidney?"

"Where to, madam?" Sid said in a voice loud enough for Zarchin to hear.

" '21,' of course," Margaret replied.

Eleven

MARGARET PRESSED HER FACE CLOSER TO the Cyclone fence, close enough to touch the warm metal with her nose, and peered through at the ten young bodies hurtling across the playground's asphalt. It took her several seconds to spot her young friend Pedro, who at that exact moment was driving in for a lay-up. The basketball spun around the rim once and grudgingly dropped through the bare hoop.

"Good shot," Margaret shouted.

"Hey." The tall Puerto Rican boy turned around to see who it was. "Margaret, hang on. Four more points and we got these suckers."

She watched as Pedro swerved down the court. Five minutes later the game was over. He made the last points with a jump shot from the corner. All his teammates came over to exchange open-handed fives and tens, and it was a few more minutes before he made his way through the gate and over to Margaret. She held out her hand palm upward as Pedro had taught her, and grinned as he gently slapped her five.

"You see that last shot?" he asked, out of breath.

"I'll never understand why you always jump in the air," she said lightly. "So unsteady. You'd think it would be better with your feet planted firmly on the ground." She looked up at his handsome features; he had always reminded her of a young Ramon Novarro, and she touched his arm. "How have you been, Pedro? I haven't seen you in weeks."

"Hey, I know," he said. He looked at her closely. "You okay?"

She nodded. "I'm kind of on a job again, like the last one, remember. . . . It's keeping me tied up."

"Yeah, I remember." Pedro grinned. "You had me worried there for a while who you was going to finger."

"I never suspected you for a minute." She laughed. "Come on." She put her arm through his. "Walk with me for a few blocks. I want to ask you something." He raised an eyebrow. "Well, actually, Jerry's waiting," she continued. "I was hoping the two of you boys would do me a favor."

"Uh huh." Pedro wrapped the towel around his neck and bent low enough to look Margaret right in the eye. "No risk, of course?" he asked. "I got a good job now."

"That depends," she replied, "on how fast you are."

Jerry Stein was supposed to be waiting for them at the coffee shop. Margaret had left him fifteen minutes earlier happily settled over a cup of coffee and the daily chess puzzle. But as they walked in, he was nowhere in sight, the table had been cleared off, and a stranger was sitting in his place. Margaret shook her head in surprise and gave Pedro an apologetic shrug. She felt a tap on her shoulder and turned to see a middle-aged blonde who was working on a piece of gum as though her life depended on it. The small apron she was wearing did little to cover several days' worth of coffee splatters on her tight uniform.

"Your name Binton?" she asked. It came out as vacantly as if she were asking, "How'd you like the eggs?"

Margaret nodded. The waitress pointed lazily out the window and up the street.

"Told me to tell you he was over there. Got tired of waiting."

Margaret looked through the window for a moment and then with confusion over to Pedro.

"Bagel Nosh," he supplied. "They got an Asteroid over there." He motioned, and she followed him out.

"Asteroid?" She couldn't imagine what he was talking about. She was still wondering as they made their way into the other restaurant. The smell of fresh bagels hung in the air like a wet blanket. There were only a few people eating at the tables, but Jerry was not one of them. She noticed a small knot of people standing around an electronic game in one of the corners of the room. She took two steps closer and saw a short young man with his hands on the controls. His eyes had the concentration of a pilot bringing down a crippled jet in a crosswind. There was a beading of sweat on his forehead, and his body jerked in response to the movements of his hands. But Margaret noticed the tight little grin on his face and chuckled to herself. She took a few steps closer and edged in next to Jerry.

"Giving up chess?" she whispered.

"That you, Margaret?" Jerry asked, not taking his eyes from the video screen. In front of him an electronic asteroid was closing in on the single spaceship. Jerry pushed a button, and a flash of white light streaked from the nose of the rocket and blasted the asteroid into a dozen harmless particles.

"Who else?" she replied. "I thought we were going to talk. Pedro's here."

"Not now. There's ten dollars says I can't break fifty thousand." Jerry blasted another two asteroids and just moved the rocket in time to miss a collision with a third. Margaret looked at the score. It was fifty-one thousand.

"You've won," she said.

"And another ten if I go the hundred."

Margaret shrugged and looked around the small group of onlookers. It was easy to spot Jerry's current victim, a young man in a jogger's outfit with an annoyed look on his face. It was the same expression of disbelief and disgust she'd seen on the faces of people Jerry had hustled in Ping-Pong and in pool up at Game City. But Asteroids was new. She wondered when he'd found the time to practice.

"I'll be sitting down," she said and turned away. Pedro followed, and they found a booth by the front window.

In five minutes they heard a light spattering of applause and a minute later Jerry came over with a satisfied look on his face. There was a twenty-dollar bill in his left hand.

"A hundred, twenty-four thousand six hundred," he said with a sigh as he sat down. "The machine high." He smiled expansively. "Listen, whyntcha have a bagel . . . my treat."

Margaret looked at him steadily for a few seconds.

"I will," she said finally. "Cream cheese and Nova on a poppy seed." Pedro got up to get it, snatching the twenty from between Jerry's fingers. "Don't forget the tomato and onion," she cried after him. She leaned forward to take a sip of her coffee. "Hustling video games now?" Margaret asked without looking up. There was just the slightest hint of disapproval in her voice.

"Hey, I tried, Margaret," Jerry said. "I told you I got a job running down on Wall Street. Entry-level, work-my-way-up sort of stuff. Took me all of two weeks to see what a fraud that was. Investment counseling." He laughed. "All it is is hustling on a grand scale. The jerks on the end of the phones get taken by half a point a trade, the brokers go home fat and smug, and I was doing twenty-eight dollars a day minus carfare. That's about an hour's work for me up at Game City." He shook his head. "Uh-unh, respectability was costing me about a hundred and a half a day. I couldn't afford it. Besides"—he looked over at the asteroid machine—"there's always some new game in town. Keeps things interesting."

Margaret looked up at Jerry. For all his experienced talk, his face still had a fresh innocence to it. There was a layer of baby fat to his ruddy cheeks, and his eyelashes were long enough to syndicate. He wore his dark hair in a Jewish afro, naturally curly and overgrowing everything, stopping just short of his Buddy Holly black frame glasses. The effect of all this was to make him appear quite harmless. She sighed and made room in front of her for the plate Pedro was bringing over. "Anyway, thanks for the bagel," she said.

"Bagel," Jerry snorted, looking at the heaping sandwich and all the fixings. "I ate worse at my bar mitzvah."

"Pobre niño," Pedro said, sitting down with his own sandwich. He held his hand out with the change.

Jerry pocketed the money and looked at Margaret. "Now, what's this all about?"

She fussed around with the onion for a minute, getting it placed just right on the slabs of smoked salmon. Then she took a bite and waited until she was finished chewing.

"I would like," she began softly, "for you two boys to borrow something for me."

"Borrow?" Pedro raised an eyebrow.

"As in five-finger discount," Jerry added. "Sounds like that's what she means."

"Well, to be precise, yes." She blushed. "It would be, uh . . . unauthorized. But it shouldn't be too difficult; it's not something big like a car."

"Cars are easy," Pedro interjected. "I got a cousin on De Kalb Avenue. You place an order with him, say for a seventy-nine white Buick Electra, and the next week it's in front of your door."

"Yeah, along with the cops," Jerry said.

"No way, man."

Margaret held up a hand. "We're not talking about cars; we're talking about dimes."

"Dimes?" Both boys said it at the same time. "Dimes?"

"Yes, I need a Liberty Seated 1871 CC just for a few hours." She looked guilty. "They're rather expensive, and it's only for a short time so . . ."

"So, you wanted us to take one," Jerry said. "I don't believe I'm hearing this right. And you're the one wanted me to quit hustling."

"It's very important," Margaret said quickly. "Believe me, I wouldn't ask you if I didn't think it was absolutely necessary. Besides, we'll send it right back afterward."

"Why do you want it?" Pedro asked.

She looked at him closely. "I can't tell you. You'll have to trust me." After a second of silence Pedro shrugged and bit into his bagel.

"But, Margaret," Jerry continued. "How are we going to get a rare coin, even for a few hours?"

She smiled as she reached into her purse. "I think I can help you there. At least it's a start." She pulled out a small coin and put it down on the table. "An 1871 Liberty Seated dime, not minted at Carson City. I just bought it from a local dealer for ten dollars. It's the same in every way but the mint mark."

Jerry picked it up and inspected the coin. Then he put it in his palm and slowly turned his hand over. His hand remained flat, but the coin didn't fall. "Margaret, you came to the right place."

"That's it," Margaret said with delight.

"An old trick I picked up waiting for a table at Game City. It's a thumb palm. Works for anything smaller than a quarter. If you do it just right, you can turn your hand front and back, even wiggle your five fingers, and the coin remains hidden." He showed them. Then he moved his thumb, and they could see the dime held in place by one of the fleshy wrinkles at its base.

"That's good," Pedro said slowly, "but only for bringing

the fake in unexpected. Palming the real one will be spotted.''

"Yeah," Jerry said with a grin. "But there's more, watch." He held the coin between his thumb and middle finger and slightly bent his wrist downward. Then, in a movement that was as quick as it was unexpected, Jerry snapped his fingers as though he were calling for a hot dog at a ball game. When he opened his hand again, the coin was gone.

"Hey," Pedro said. "Do that again." He looked on the floor. "Where'd it go?"

"Up the much-maligned sleeve," Jerry said. He shook it out of his jacket.

"Damn, that's nice." Pedro whistled.

"And it's so fast you absolutely can't see it. That's the best part," Jerry said.

"You ever miss?" Margaret asked.

"One in three," Jerry said sheepishly, and sure enough on the next try the coin hit the cuff of his jacket and bounced back onto the tabletop. "But if I practice I can do better."

Margaret finished the last bit of her bagel and sat back with an unlit cigarette. "You have to get it perfect." She looked at Pedro. "And you'll need to do something to distract the dealer while Jerry makes the switch."

Pedro smiled. "That's easy. I'll work something out." He turned to Jerry. "What do you say, wanna try it?"

"For Margaret?" His eyes sparkled behind the black frame glasses. "I'd consider it an honor. Just tell us where to go."

Margaret took a list out of her handbag. "These are some of the dealers downtown. Several of them should have an 1871 CC, but try and find one whose coin has the same look, the same patina as the fake."

"I understand." Jerry nodded and put the fake in his wallet. "When do you want it?"

"Tomorrow," Margaret said.

Jerry gave Pedro a quick glance and saw the tiny nod.

"Lunchtime I can make it."

"Okay," Jerry said, "if everything goes all right we'll have the coin for you around one thirty, two."

"And if it doesn't?" Pedro said lightly.

"She'll have to pay for her own lunch."

Twelve

IT WAS ALREADY ONE FIFTEEN BY THE TIME Jerry walked out of the fourth dealer's office. He looked dejectedly at Pedro waiting by the elevator and shook his head.

"No dice," Jerry said. "He's got one, but it's too shiny. Spot it in a minute."

"Least he's got one," Pedro said angrily.

Jerry consulted a scrap of paper he had in his pocket. He was wearing his only suit, a blue corduroy made in Rumania and purchased by him for his brief flirtation with Wall Street. Today he was even wearing a tie.

"There's one more dealer in the building," Jerry noted. "On five." They got on the elevator, dropped two floors, and emerged onto a long corridor. The building they were in housed dozens of small, one-room concerns: camera repair services, import/export brokers, semiprecious-stone merchants . . . businesses that didn't mind chickenwire glass with chipping gold-leaf signs on their front doors and dim airless hallways. A strong smell of disinfectant greeted them as they passed the men's room.

"Wait here," Jerry said and went looking for room 508, home of Kleinman's Coin Company. He found it around a bend in the corridor, rang the bell, and waited. Nothing happened. He rang a second time and knocked on the glass, but still there was no response. He was about to turn away when he heard the scrape of a shoe behind the door, and then the click of a lock being pulled back. The door opened and Jerry saw an older man with a gray mustache and a felt hat. A cigarette dangled from a corner of his mouth, and smoke coiled up around the features of his face. Behind wire-rim glasses his moist eyes squinted at Jerry speculatively.

"Can I help you?" he asked, not stepping back into his shop.

"Good afternoon," Jerry said amiably. "I'm just in from Boston and I was told that you're one of the better dealers in New York. I'm trying to secure an 1871 CC Seated Liberty dime for my collection. Nothing under 'extremely fine,' of course."

The man gave Jerry a quick once over and stepped back. "Yes, I got one. Ain't cheap, though."

"So I understand," Jerry said, following him in.

The dealer stepped behind a glass-topped counter and motioned for Jerry to wait. He went into a back room and in another minute emerged with a small leather-bound book. Jerry watched as he thumbed through the pages and finally stopped near the end.

"An 1871 CC," he said, holding out a coin in a little plastic envelope. "I class it an AU-fifty . . . almost uncirculated. Four thousand without the sales tax."

Jerry studied it closely. As far as he could tell, the coin was in good condition, but what was even better, it had almost the exact patina as the one in his pocket. Jerry coughed twice, the signal to Pedro, and asked politely if he could take the coin out of the envelope.

"By the edges," the dealer said.

"Of course," Jerry answered brusquely, as though it were an insult to suggest something so basic. He took his left hand out of his pocket, slid the coin out of the envelope, and lifted it up to eye level. In the crease between his thumb and index finger was the duplicate. He tilted the coin back and forth for a few seconds and frowned. "Four thousand, you say?"

"That's right, cash."

There was a knock on the door and the dealer looked up with annoyance. "Friend of yours?" he asked.

Jerry shook his head. Very quickly the dealer rounded the counter, opened the door, and looked back at Jerry. In the three seconds his eyes were averted, Jerry made the switch. The 1871 CC flew up his sleeve as smoothly as a nesting sparrow and the ten-dollar coin took its position securely between Jerry's fingers. This was accomplished without any noticeable movement on Jerry's part; just a little "snap" sounded which went unheard in the wake of Pedro's bellowed "Okay, where is she!"

Mr. Kleinman, looking shocked, retreated behind his counter.

"Evangeline," Pedro said angrily. "I know she works here, man. She's trying to give me the runaround. Bitch owes me sixty dollars. . . ."

The dealer, without taking his eyes off the coin, was now shaking his head vigorously.

"No Evangeline here," he said. "You've got the wrong place."

Jerry very deliberately slid the coin back into the plastic envelope and put it gently on the counter in front of him. The dealer put a hand out for it anxiously and, as he touched it, looked up at Pedro with more assurance.

"I know she's here, pop," the young boy was saying. "In that room behind you."

"It's very nice," Jerry said. "But not worth four thousand. I can offer you three, maybe thirty-one. No more."

"Wait a minute," the dealer said and protectively put the coin back into the book, snapping the cover shut.

"Evangeline," Pedro shouted. "Get your ass out here!"

"Hey, how about it," Jerry said, looking with annoyance at Pedro. He turned back to the dealer. "This happen a lot with your employees?"

"There's no Evangeline working here!" the dealer shouted. "There's no one here but me, goddammit. This man is crazy."

"Ain't this a coin place?" Pedro asked menacingly. "Evangeline told me she worked in a coin place in this building."

"There are three other coin shops in this building," the dealer yelled. "Maybe one of them has an Evangeline. I don't. Now, get the hell out of here—"

Pedro took a breath.

"—before I call the cops," the dealer continued.

"Okay, man." Pedro backed away. "Sorry, keep your shirt on." He turned and slipped back out.

"So," Jerry continued. "How about the thirty-one?"

The dealer stared absently at Jerry for a few seconds, then came to life. "Oh, the 1871 CC. No, not under four."

"Thirty-one fifty, that's my last," Jerry said, reaching for his back pocket.

"Forget it. This isn't a vegetable market. You want the coin, it's yours for four."

Jerry shook his head and shrugged.

"Perhaps after I look around," he said and turned to go. "Thanks anyway." He walked through the door and turned to the elevators. Before the door closed he saw Kleinman heading toward his back room with the book.

"So," he said to Pedro when they met downstairs. "You find Evangeline?"

"Ha." Pedro smiled. "Musta been the wrong address."

"Not me," Jerry said and brought out the 1871 CC dime from his back pocket. "I just hope it doesn't become habit forming."

Thirteen

FRENOS ZARCHIN'S SHOP WAS LOCATED in the West Seventies off Riverside Drive. From the outside there was no evidence that the elegant Victorian town house was not a multiple residence like the dozens of others that lined the side streets in that neighborhood. But once inside the front door, Margaret realized immediately that it was one of the few that was still private. There was a thick maroon-and-cream-colored oriental rug in the foyer. Where the ubiquitous row of stainless-steel mailboxes should have been was an ornately gilded beveled glass mirror above a Louis XIV side table. A marble staircase rose in front of her in a graceful curve to the second floor. She stood awkwardly waiting for the housekeeper who had opened the door to direct her. Then she saw a man descending the staircase.

"Mrs. Sloan, right on time," Zarchin said as he held out a hand. "I was so delighted when you called. Do come in."

Margaret gave him a charming little smile and let him lead her through a door on her left. She found herself in a large double parlor with high ceilings. She noticed that all the little details of molding and woodwork were perfectly intact, but that instead of parlor-type furnishings, there was a mahogany-inlaid desk in a corner with two chairs beside it. The only other objects in the room were either freestanding or wall showcases. It reminded Margaret of an intimate cul-de-sac in a museum. The parquet floor was exposed and highly polished.

"Sit down, please," Zarchin said, indicating one of the chairs by the desk. "This is my little shop." He gestured. "As you can see, everything is nicely displayed. Quite often people come just to sell and wind up going home with new coins for their collections."

Margaret looked on the wall to the left of her and saw some small old coins. She leaned closer, held her glasses out an inch from her nose, and studied them closely.

"My staters," Zarchin said.

"Lydian," Margaret replied, replacing her glasses. "However, the fact that they're from 700 B.C. does not alter the precarious nature of collecting them. One sizeable find . . ." She shrugged her shoulders and smiled. "You understand."

Zarchin nodded. "So far I've been lucky." He leaned back in his chair, lifted a pipe from an ashtray on the desk, and carefully filled it from a silver repoussé humidor. "Tell me, Mrs. Sloan. You did say scrap metal?" He looked closely at her. "I mean what your husband did."

"Yes," Margaret said and quickly turned to look at the other showcases. "Uh . . . Puerto Rican scrap metal. He always said there was a fortune to be made down there."

"I see," Zarchin said thoughtfully. He puffed up a cloud of fragrant smoke. After a minute he offered politely, "Please do look around."

"Are those Maria Theresa thalers?" Margaret asked, not getting up. "My eyes aren't what they used to be."

Zarchin allowed a tiny smile to cross his face.

"They're good enough. Yes, they're thalers. I suppose I should apologize for having them, but every now and then I get someone who would like a pretty coin for under a hundred dollars. They're like loss leaders, if you know what I mean."

"I do." Margaret frowned and turned back. "Mr. Zarchin, I'll be blunt. Surely you don't have your real collection out here. The Augustus Humbert, for example." She raised an eyebrow.

Zarchin studied her for a minute without saying anything.

The smile that was on his face seemed painted there. Only the sounds of his sucking on the pipe stem interrupted the silence.

"No," he said at last. "The Humbert is not out here. Nor is the 1822 Half Eagle. Security reasons." Margaret waited, but all he did was lean back in the chair and watch her closely.

"I see." Margaret sighed at last and looked at the cloud of smoke over the dealer's head. "I don't suppose you mind if I smoke?" she asked, changing the subject.

"Not at all." Zarchin leaned forward with his lighter ready. Margaret fished busily in her handbag for a cigarette. The bag was crammed with miscellaneous items, and, as she groped lower, she removed some of them and put them on the desk in front of her. A comb came out, then a compact, a set of keys, and finally a handkerchief.

"Here they are," she said, holding up the pack of Dunhills. But Zarchin's eyes were riveted to the comb and the little coin stuck between its plastic teeth.

"Is that . . ." he began and reached out his hand slowly.

"Oh, my," Margaret fussed. "It must have rolled out of the handkerchief."

"An 1871 CC dime." Zarchin studied it, holding it carefully by the edges. "Not something you want casually rolling around in the bottom of a handbag, Mrs. Sloan." He handed it back to her slowly and she carefully wrapped it in the handkerchief.

"How silly of me," she said. "I was looking for that this morning." She smiled with embarrassment. "Just something I picked up earlier this week." She put the handkerchief in her breast pocket. "Now I shall surely remember." She put the cigarette in her mouth and leaned forward. Zarchin flicked his lighter and Margaret inhaled deeply. Neither spoke for a few moments as Margaret repacked her handbag.

"So," she continued. "You were saying . . . about security. I do understand. One must be extra careful these days." She tapped an ash off into the agate ashtray and leaned back. "But surely, Mr. Zarchin, you do understand I didn't come to see 'loss leaders,' as you call them."

Zarchin looked at her quickly and seemed to make a decision. He knocked the dottle out of his pipe and put it down.

"No, of course not. I just thought you'd like to start here." He got up and held out her chair. "Perhaps we should go right away to the real collection. If you'll follow me." He held the door open and led her past the marble staircase to a small private elevator set in an alcove. There was just enough room inside for the two of them, and even then Margaret was so close she could smell the faint aroma of Zarchin's pipe tobacco on his breath.

"This is my upstairs study," Zarchin said as the elevator came to a halt on the second floor. Margaret saw before her a tiny foyer and a closed glass door. She reached for the doorknob, but Zarchin stopped her. He took a key out and inserted it in an unobtrusive keyhole inside the elevator.

"Heat sensors," he said. "When it's armed even a little cat walking around will set it off." He preceded her into the room and pulled out another key. He hurried to a little box a few feet away and clicked it in. "And sonar. Rings directly to Pinkerton. One can't be too careful. Now," he said with a smile, "please come in."

Margaret took a step into the room and stopped short. Zarchin's study took up the entire second floor and measured thirty by fifty feet. It was so large that it reminded her of the lobby of the New Yorker Theater, except that the New Yorker didn't have hundreds of mysterious and lovely artifacts displayed in such profusion. Malachite and lapis lazuli inlaid clocks vied with Chinese porcelain vases for table space. The furniture was all Victorian and exquisitely preserved. Two wisteria Tiffany lamps framed a seven-foot medallion-back finger-carved sofa. Two gentleman's walnut smoking chairs in pale-olive crushed velvet faced the sofa across the large expanse of a nineteenth-century palace Sirouk rug. The walls held several framed paintings under little display lights. Margaret recognized one, a small Monet watercolor. But what caught her attention immediately was the facing wall on which Zarchin again had several display cases. The largest case held over two dozen stilettos and daggers, each beautifully forged and jeweled. Without thinking Margaret walked over to it and looked more closely.

"Sort of a little hobby," Zarchin said behind her. "What you see there are only my best." He pointed to one in the center. "That one is a silver kriss from Indonesia, presumably the very knife that a fifteenth-century Buddhist monk committed suicide with. To get that I had to trade almost a dozen of my best seventeenth-century Japanese tsuba."

"They're all beautiful," Margaret said casually and turned away. "But while I can appreciate their appeal to you, personally they make me quite uncomfortable." She took out her pack of Dunhills again and held it ready. "I would really love to see the coins, Mr. Zarchin."

"Yes, the coins," he said, smiling. "Please, they are this way." Margaret was shown to the couch where she politely waited while Zarchin went to his safe. The Monet swung out on hidden hinges and revealed a gray steel door. Recessed in the center was a set of electronic buttons. Zarchin punched the top one and then moved so as to block Margaret's vision. He waited a second, then tapped out a code on the keyboard. Immediately a click was heard, and the steel door was released. Zarchin reached in, pulled out a leather-bound portfolio, closed the safe, and walked over to the couch.

"It's not often I do this," he said with delight. "But then again, it's not often you meet someone with such similar interests in coins. Here is the collection," he said almost reverently, and put it down on the ornate teak carved side table at her elbow. "I believe it is, as you said, quite extraordinary. I think you'll agree after seeing it." He sat on the couch next to her and watched carefully. His face settled into a kind of smug grin as she slowly turned the lettered pages.

And for a moment Margaret forgot why she was there. In the several weeks of intensive study she had come to feel something of the excitement of coin collecting. She delighted at reading the strange histories of the various rare coins, and marveled at their exquisite detailed beauty. But the illustrations in the books were faded reproductions compared to the actual coins she was now holding. She nearly gasped several

times, especially at the 1822 Half Eagle, which was in flaw-
less mint condition. Zarchin's collection had many of the
rarest coins. He even had one of the five 1913 Liberty Head
nickels. All told, Margaret must have been holding several
million dollars' worth of coins. But more than their cost,
each coin represented a successful campaign of acquisition.
What manipulations and backroom dealings Zarchin must
have practiced to amass his collection she could only guess
at. Just to possess one 1913 Liberty Head nickel, she thought,
would have been a life's work. Nonetheless, Margaret closed
the folio slowly and, composing herself, looked up casually
at Zarchin. He had an expectant expression on his face.

"It's very nice," she said lightly. "Quite interesting."
Zarchin waited for more, but Margaret just leaned back into
the couch.

"Interesting?" Zarchin said finally with a trace of hostility
in his voice. "Mrs. Sloan, that's like calling the Sistine
Chapel 'colorful.' Surely you recognized several of the coins
as being priceless."

"Oh, indeed, Mr. Zarchin, and I meant no disrespect. It
is a fine collection. It's just that I was hoping to see something truly unique. After all," she said, smiling coyly, "there
is only one Sistine Chapel, isn't there?" She lit one of the
Dunhills casually and tossed the match into a brass ashtray
in the shape of a swan. "Mind you," she added quickly,
"you do have some wonderful pieces. The 1822 is lovely."
She took a puff on the cigarette and watched the smoke coil
lazily up to the coffered ceiling. "But I did hope that I was
going to see something like the Maximus I Herculius." She
shrugged. "You know, the only one, hidden away for cen-
turies . . . the stuff of fantasy, Mr. Zarchin." She sighed.
"I guess Cornelius was right. He always said I was a roman-
tic at heart."

She looked straight at the red-haired collector without
blinking. "These days, I guess such uniqueness is impossible outside of museums." There was a silence so pervasive
Margaret thought she could hear her blood racing. Zarchin

held her stare for several seconds and finally reached out for the leather book.

"Nothing is impossible," he said softly, "if you know how to go about it. I have at times exceeded even some of these pieces . . . certain acquisitions . . . which I never show . . . things truly unique." His words were now coming more slowly, as though they were struggling to free themselves. "Coins to make you weep," he finally said, not much above a whisper.

"Exactly," Margaret said, crushing out her cigarette.

"Weep!" he exclaimed suddenly and got up. "I'll show you." He rushed over to the safe and almost haphazardly pushed back the leather book, flinging the door shut behind it. Then he walked quickly to another picture on the wall, a little Renaissance drawing, and swung it forward to reveal another safe. In ten seconds he had that one open and reached in. He withdrew a small plain black case and in three steps was by her side untying the strings that kept it together.

"This," he said breathlessly, "is perhaps what you had in mind."

Margaret looked down and saw Hannah's coin. At least it had the same lady with flowing hair, the same lettering, and the same date. She even remembered to look at the edge and noted that it was unlettered as expected. The more she gazed at it, the more she was certain she'd seen that exact coin before. She tried to say something, but her voice failed her.

"What?" Zarchin snapped.

"Is that what I think it is—an 1804 dollar?" she managed. "I've never seen one."

"Not just any 1804 dollar," he said, but almost as soon as the words were out, his expression changed. A cold light came into his eyes as he watched her, and he pulled the case back and quickly retied the closures on the outside. Margaret reached out a hand to ask to see the coin again, but Zarchin was already taking his prize away. He closed the safe behind it and swung the drawing back in place.

"Would you like some tea?" he asked quickly, as though the last minute and a half had never happened.

"But, Mr. Zarchin, why tease me? That was an 1804 dollar, wasn't it?" Margaret asked. "And what did you mean 'not just any one'?"

"Just talk," he said, trying to sound casual. There was an awkward silence for a few seconds. Finally he came over and sat down next to her. "You must forgive me, Mrs. Sloan. I've never shown it before. I'm apt to be a little nervous. . . . You understand."

Margaret laughed. "Surely, Mr. Zarchin, you don't think I'd steal it?"

He studied her carefully, then passed off her remark with a relieved grin. "If you did, Mrs. Sloan, it would be one of the most foolish and self-destructive acts you've ever done. The tea?"

Margaret shook her head. "But where did you get it?" she asked, trying to sound innocent. "I don't recall you being listed as an owner."

Zarchin laughed, but to Margaret it sounded hollow and forced. "Privately." He pulled out his pipe and relit it. "Can you keep a secret, Mrs. Sloan?"

She nodded.

"Well, then, I'll tell you. The previous owner needed two things: a lot of money and anonymity. The sale was never recorded because he would have had to pay a huge capital gains tax. As far as the IRS is concerned, he still owns it. If they ask to see it, he'll have it. But when he dies they'll find our legal sale papers and I suspect by then they'll have a hard time finding their tax." He leaned forward. "You see, the gentleman in question plans to build a most lavish retirement home on the Costa Del Sol." He winked and slowly sank back into the couch. "And that's why I must be very careful to whom I show the coin."

"I see," Margaret answered, and she looked casually at her watch. "Oh, my, it's late. I really must be running along. I do appreciate everything, including that all-too-brief look at the 1804." She leaned closer and lowered her voice. "And don't worry. I won't say a word about it. I, too, understand these tax matters." She grabbed her handbag and stood up.

"I'd love to stay longer and chat, but I have this silly luncheon appointment at the Ford Foundation. Want me on a committee or something." She took a few steps in the direction of the elevator. "Quite transparent. All they want is another donation." She shrugged and continued across the room. Zarchin followed. "One thing puzzles me," Margaret said, turning back. "Why two safes?"

Zarchin smiled. "I find anything that's worth doing once is worth duplicating. Call it contingency planning."

"I noticed," Margaret said, watching him rearm the sonar security system on the wall.

"I'll see you out," he said cordially and got in the tiny elevator after her. The door closed slowly, trapping Margaret and Zarchin inside. She gave a little shudder and looked up at the dealer, now only a few inches away. Unexpectedly Zarchin put his hand on her shoulder, near her neck, and pressed lightly. It was not a friendly gesture.

"I would appreciate your discretion," he said slowly. "You do understand."

Margaret swallowed hard and nodded twice. "Of course."

The door opened and Zarchin backed out. Margaret walked past him to the front door.

"About those staters," she managed on her way out. "I'd really get rid of them. You're playing with fire there."

"Sometimes it pays to take risks," he said coldly as he closed the door gently behind her.

Fourteen

THE LIMOUSINE PULLED SLOWLY UP THE circular driveway leading to the white columned house. The grounds on either side of the road were immaculately groomed. A sloping lawn gave a long, expansive view past flowering dogwood to the gatehouse at the entrance to the estate. But Zarchin shifted uneasily in the back of the car. These million-dollar houses, the servants, the swimming pools and saunas, were all window dressing. At heart he knew the men he was dealing with had the taste and elegance of hundred-dollar hoods. The only difference was his New Jersey friends had been at it longer.

"Here we are, Mr. Zarchin," the sleepy-looking chauffeur said into the rearview mirror. "The boss said he'd be waiting for you in the den."

Zarchin got out of the car and walked through the open door. The door was always open, he remembered, under the assumption that robbing that particular house was as efficient an act of suicide as you could get without a razor. Zarchin moved to the den and stepped into its heavy fake Edwardian ambience. The first time he'd been summoned he'd made the mistake of pulling a leather-bound copy of *Crime and Punishment* off the shelf. Along with Dostoyevsky's great work seven other hollow pieces of bound plywood had come with it.

"Good afternoon, Frenos," the other occupant of the room said. "I'm glad you're so prompt." He held out his hand and took the three steps to the dealer's side. "A nice trait."

Zarchin took the hand and looked appraisingly at its owner. Five foot five had never been an advantageous height for a full-grown male, but then it had never been a liability for Zarchin's host either. The man standing in front of him packed more nervous determination and hard-edged authority into his undersized frame than Zarchin had encountered in men half again as big. Zarchin only knew him as Mr. Contini. He wasn't sure he wanted to know more.

"I'm always prompt," Zarchin said and reached slowly into his breast pocket. Before he could remove his hand with the envelope, he felt something cold at the base of his skull.

"Ain't necessary, Wayne," the short man said. "Frenos knows better."

Zarchin turned, still with his hand inside his jacket, and found himself staring the wrong way down the barrel of a 9mm Walther PPK. On the other end was the very silent chauffeur.

"In fact, kid, whyntcha beat it. We got some business to do." The short man nodded, and the chauffeur left as silently as he had entered. "Hey, I apologize," Zarchin's host said. "He's a new boy and a little overprotective." He gestured to a desk at one side of the room. "Sit." Zarchin followed him, took his hand out of his pocket, and tossed the envelope he'd been reaching for on the soft green felt of the desktop. It was the kind of felt used to seeing money come and go . . . crap-table felt.

"The coins were sent to Degia in Scottsdale under your name last week. There's the summary," Zarchin said as he eased himself into a nearby chair. He watched as the short man unfolded the two pieces of paper and slowly read the numbers.

"Eight hundred thousand?" Mr. Contini said matter-of-factly.

"That's what Degia paid for them and that's what I could get from any dealer anywhere. There were some nice coins in the lot. Besides, Degia's discreet, I'm out there enough to know.''

''What the hell do I care what they were?'' the short man said. ''Could be plug nickels.'' He opened his top drawer and pressed a button. A door clicked open on the wall behind him and a whole section of books swung outward. In two minutes he had the concealed safe opened and an enormous roll of cash in his hands. He counted out three hundred thousand dollars and handed it across the desk. Then he pulled out a checkbook and wrote out a check for a half million dollars. He stapled his check to the second piece of paper, Zarchin's formal invoice for five hundred thousand dollars, and also handed those across the desk.

''There,'' he said. ''Five on top and three under. Eight in all. When do I get paid from Degia?''

Zarchin smiled. ''As soon as you send him your bill for the full eight on your personal letterhead. Same procedure as before.'' Zarchin counted the cash slowly. ''And just like before you show a quick, legal three hundred thousand dollars profit by doing nothing more than signing your name.''

''Yeah,'' growled the other man, ''and also give you a three hundred grand paper tax deduction for selling your coins at a loss. That ain't nothing to sneeze at.''

Zarchin stopped his count and looked up.

''You're forgetting I have to deal with someone else's tainted money.'' He held up the clump of greenbacks. ''How many people you know can launder as much as I do . . . and as often?''

The short man shrugged. ''In your business . . . you just go out and buy a few more little coins, pay cash, put them away. What's so hard about that?''

Zarchin went back to his count. ''That's right, just go out and buy a few little coins.'' He smiled to himself as he continued shuffling through the bills. When he finished he put them into his side pocket and leaned back. ''Thank you,'' he said. ''All there.'' He looked around the room. When his eyes came back to rest on the man across from him he frowned for a moment. ''You mind if I ask you a question?

Nothing personal.'' The other man shrugged. ''You once told me you knew someone in scrap metal?''

''Yeah, a buddy of mine from the early years. He went his way, I went mine.'' He snorted derisively. ''Can you believe the guy's a millionaire on broken faucets and old radiators?'' He narrowed his eyes. ''Why?''

''Call him up and ask him something for me.''

''Important?''

''Maybe.''

The shorter man thought for a moment and then leaned over his desk and reached for the phone. In fifteen seconds he had someone on the other end. After a greeting he leaned in Zarchin's direction. ''What do you want?''

''Ask if he's ever heard of Cornelius Sloan, an important man in Puerto Rican scrap metal. Died maybe a year or two ago.'' He leaned back and heard his question repeated into the phone. Then he waited while the answer came back. After a minute Mr. Contini covered the receiver and frowned at Zarchin.

''Leo says you're crazy. Ain't never was a Sloan in Puerto Rican scrap. And Leo should know. You sure you got the right name?''

''Yeah, I got the right name,'' Zarchin said. ''But I think I got a wrong number. Very wrong!''

Fifteen

THE ONLY STOP MARGARET MADE BE-
tween Zarchin's house and the precinct was at a mailbox to

send the 1871 CC back to Mr. Kleinman. When she rushed in, Morley was over by the rusty hot plate near the water cooler. He had been standing there patiently for over two minutes waiting for the little kettle to boil. It was an afternoon ritual, his four P.M. coffee break. Margaret hadn't checked in with the desk sergeant. She had swiftly threaded her way through the group of policemen and assorted patrons straight toward Morley. A wisp of steam escaped from the kettle lid as she tugged at his elbow.

"I told you I'd find it," she began.

Morley turned and saw Margaret standing there like someone who had just yelled "BINGO" at a church bazaar. He looked her over casually and then went back to listening for the telltale screech of the kettle.

"Did you hear?" she continued. "I found the coin."

"Mmmm," Morley said and debated whether to pour the water yet. "What coin?" he asked absently, concentrating now on what he thought might be the beginning of the whistle.

"Sam Morley," she said, fuming. "You're not listening. Or you're just trying to be difficult. The 1804, of course. The one I told you Zarchin has." Margaret heard the shrill whistle and looked down.

"Have some tea?" Morley offered and lifted the kettle off the hot plate. "Then you can tell me all about it." He splashed some boiling water into two cups, put a spoon of Nescafé into one and a tea bag into the other, and started back into his office. "Now," he said, after putting her cup down, "start again." He leaned back and cradled his own cup in his hands.

Margaret detailed her visit with Zarchin. Midway through she picked up her tea and took a perfunctory sip, but her heart wasn't in it. She was too engrossed in her story. When she'd finished, she searched Morley's desk and finally saw the pack of Camels poking out from under a mess of papers. She lit one and waited.

"Interesting," Morley said somewhat coolly. He fidgeted for a moment, then finally looked up at Margaret. "For your information, I had Shaeffer check on this guy. You want to hear?''

She shrugged. "What's it matter?"

"Plenty." Morley took a swallow. "This is no little two-bit coin dealer you hooked onto. That's one area of his interests, but he's also considered one of the shrewdest option and commodity traders by Wall Streeters who know." Morley sighed. "The man is worth a lot of money and"—he hesitated—"has enough close ties with a North Jersey crime family to warrant an investigation. But he's just been too insulated by smart lawyers and important friends." Morley drank the last of his coffee and put the cup on the windowsill behind him. "The DA tangled with him once, but it almost cost him his job. Witnesses all backed down at the last minute. . . . That's your man."

Margaret narrowed her eyes and crushed out the cigarette.

"I guess it is," she said in a voice that carried all the defiance she could muster. There was silence while they looked at each other carefully. "Lieutenant Morley, I don't think I like where this is heading," she continued. "If you're suggesting just because Zarchin is a wealthy man . . ."

"I'm suggesting this might be too big for you, that's all," Morley said, grabbing angrily for his cigarettes.

"Well, there's only one way to find out, just like you promised."

Morley reddened. "I didn't promise anything. I merely agreed to look the other way."

Margaret stood up and bent slightly forward at the waist. Even then she was only a few inches above him. When she spoke, her voice was low and quite controlled.

"Samuel, you have never lied or reneged on an agreement yet. If you start now, I will lose all my respect for you. You're too good for that. You did promise, right here in front of Sergeant Shaeffer, to follow up my investigation with a legal and thorough search. You did not say you would conduct the search only if the man had a police record or only if he had assets under a thousand dollars. You agreed to the search without exceptions, and now I'm asking you to go ahead with it. And if you're worried, here's one witness that won't back down. If you refuse, I'm afraid it will have to mark the end of our friendship."

Morley looked up at her with a frown on his face. He looked at her for several seconds, then sighed. "Sit down. Tell me again where you found the damn thing!"

Margaret explained again. "And you better go tonight," she concluded.

"Yes," Morley said with resignation. "I'll start Shaeffer on it. I suppose we could have the warrant in a couple of hours." He looked at her, and this time there was a slight tinge of humor in his eyes. "You sure do pick them," he said. "Right now I'll need a signed statement from you." He pressed a button on a desk intercom. "Send Jacobson in here with an affidavit form." He looked at Margaret, then over to the wall where several of his citations were framed. "I don't believe I'm doing this," he said evenly.

"Go on." Margaret smiled. "You'll probably get a promotion for it."

"Yeah, if we get the coin," he answered. "Otherwise I'm just stirring up a hornet's nest that's going to land in a cloud on the DA's desk." He looked at her mirthlessly. "And I know just who he's going to grab for a fly swatter."

Sixteen

ZARCHIN WAS IN THE MIDDLE OF A *quenelles de brochet* in a white cream sauce when the front bell sounded. He looked up mildly disturbed and watched as

Honorée, his housekeeper, went to check the door. Even though he was not expecting anyone, it was not surprising that the bell should ring at this hour. There were several children playing on the streets after dinner, and his shiny brass button always looked inviting. He took a sip of a polite little Riesling he was trying out and went back to the quenelles. Adequate, he thought, although it needed some truffles. He planned to comment on this to Honorée, but when she returned he was surprised to see two gentlemen standing at the door of the dining room. One of them was wearing a little gold earring. Honorée was wringing her hands in frustration.

"I told them you were busy," she stammered in a heavy accent. "But they don't listen."

Zarchin put his fork down softly on the plate and leaned back.

"I generally send invitations to dinner," he said, "unless you're here to read the meter."

"Neither," Shaeffer said as he pulled out his badge and an official piece of paper. "We have reason to believe there is stolen merchandise in your possession and we've got a search warrant to cover our investigation."

"Really?" Zarchin said, raising an eyebrow. "Fascinating. Perhaps if you told me what kind of merchandise you were looking for I could be of assistance. Fur coats, stereos . . ."

"Coins," Shaeffer interjected, and there was a slight hesitation from Zarchin.

"How interesting," he said finally. He reached out. "Let me see that." He read the warrant carefully and tossed it on the table. Then he waved to seats at the side of the room while he picked up his fork again. "You may begin at any time," he smiled. "If you need my assistance, you will have to wait until after the sorbet."

Jacobson looked questioningly at Shaeffer. The bearded sergeant nodded his head politely and took a step toward the chair. "We'll wait," he said. "This won't take long. I know where to look."

Seventeen

"IT WASN'T THERE?" MARGARET SAID, looking astonished. "It had to be there; I saw it just this morning."

"He must have moved it," Shaeffer said, sinking down into Margaret's favorite easy chair. He closed his eyes for a second, rubbed his eyelids, then looked up at Margaret. He had wakened her up, and she was now dressed in a flannel bathrobe and furry burgundy slippers. Her hair was in a black net that came halfway down her forehead. Still there was no trace of sleep in her voice even though she had just let him in the door.

"Jacobson and I checked the two safes like you said," Shaeffer continued. "Nothing. I mean his collection was there, but no little black case and no 1804 dollar."

"The safe behind the pencil drawing?"

"Just where you said," Shaeffer nodded.

Margaret's mouth opened to say something, but nothing emerged. She sat down slowly in a chair next to him and shook her head.

"I don't understand."

"It's easy," Shaeffer said, and there was a trace of impatience in his voice. "You scared him, and he moved it somewhere else. Jake and I tried for another hour, but his place is too big. It could be anywhere." Shaeffer stood up. "Sorry, Margaret."

"And that's all?" Margaret said with amazement. "A polite little search and you drop it. The coin's got to be there somewhere.''

"We gave it an hour," Shaeffer repeated. "We covered the room with the safes from top to bottom." He leaned tiredly against the door. "There's got to be a dozen more rooms. See the problem? Jake called in and Morley told us to beat it.''

She looked up and squinted. "What else did he say?''

"He's trying to forget the whole thing." Shaeffer shrugged. "If Zarchin lets him. But you know how things are. Zarchin'll go a little ways with it . . . but I don't think he'll go public. Guys like that can't afford even a suggestion of wrongdoing. Morley'll come out okay." He reached for the doorknob, then turned around to face her. "There's still one problem," he said. "Zarchin knows you fingered him and might try to get even. You can still testify he showed you the coin.''

"Huh?" Margaret had been thinking of something else, but now she brought her attention back to Shaeffer.

"He might come after you," Shaeffer added.

Margaret shook her head and allowed a little grin to cross her face. "As far as he knows I'm Mrs. Cornelius Sloan, address unknown. There's no way he can trace me. I made sure of that.''

Shaeffer thought this over for a moment, then shrugged tiredly. "Well, just be careful. It's finished now. Morley sent me over to tell you." He opened the door slowly, took a step through, and smiled back at Margaret. "But don't worry about him. Come by in a few weeks with some cookies and all will be forgiven.''

But Margaret wasn't listening. She was deep in thought in the chair. She didn't even hear the door close. After another five minutes she quietly got up, turned off the light in the living room, and crawled back into bed.

Eighteen

"WHAT'S THIS ALL ABOUT?" DURSO SAID as he looked skeptically around him at the score of churning clothes-washing machines. He was seated at the end of the middle row of benches at the 87th Street Coin Op Washeteria. The six adjoining plastic molded seats were occupied by Sid, Roosa, Bertie, Rena, Pancher, and Rose. All of them were just as curious as to why they had been called together and on such a wet, miserable day. A steady rain beat against the plate-glass window of the laundry.

"Margaret asked me to bring you all," Sid began, "but she didn't say why." He looked around at the large, brightly lit laundry and shrugged. "At least it's out of the rain." Several other people were hanging around waiting for their machines to stop. No one seemed to be paying any attention to the little group. There was a sharp smell of detergent in the air and a humidity that was like an August evening. Durso frowned and looked to the door. "There she is!"

Margaret walked over, shook her umbrella off, and greeted each one warmly. They hadn't seen her in several weeks, and there were many questions. After a few moments she held up her hand, drew over an unattached chair, and sat facing them. She had to raise her voice to carry over the clattering of the machines.

"I'm glad you could all come," she began. "I'm sorry for the inconvenience. I had to see you right away." She stopped to light a cigarette. A young man passed by on his way to the soap powder dispenser. When he was back in front of his machine again, she continued. "I need your help."

Roosa nervously put two fingers down inside the little brown bag he was holding and felt reassuringly for the neck of the bottle. He edged the cap off, then brought it up quickly for a swallow. Bertie elbowed him lightly in the side and shot him her most indignant frown. He winked sheepishly and turned to look at Margaret.

"A man has committed murder," she continued. "Many of you were friends of Hannah Jansen, may she rest in peace. I thought you would want to help bring this man to justice." There was a buzzing of conversation as several of the old people leaned over to their neighbors. Margaret waited a minute and continued. "The police have backed off after the most begrudging of attempts. It seems they feel they have little chance of a conviction with him. They've tried before and failed. I suppose they have their priorities." She looked around. "But so do I. Hannah was my friend, and I will not give up. Now," she said, "let me tell you what's happened."

In ten minutes she had recounted her story up to the point where Shaeffer had done his unsuccessful search. The little group had huddled closer to Margaret and were silently hanging on to her every word. Rena Bernstein's eyes remained open without blinking, and Sid loosened his tie. Even Roosa forgot about his bottle. When she had finished, Margaret leaned back and surveyed them carefully. Durso was the first to speak.

"But what can we do?" he asked. "The coin is gone."

"Yes, and without that we have no case," Margaret said. "There's only one thing left to do, and that is to pressure him into telling us where he hid it."

"Pressure him." Sid laughed. "You're kidding. How are you going to pressure a man that's got money like that? If you go to the press, he'll throw a libel suit at you." He grabbed for a cigar and stuck it in his mouth. "That's the trouble. Bunch of old people like us got no power . . . and never did."

"I dunno," Pancher said, casually rubbing his white stubble beard. "We come through good last time."

"Rose," Margaret said after a minute. "You know this area like it was your own living room." She looked at the timid, disheveled lady with her five stuffed shopping bags. Rose looked up and flashed a gap-toothed smile of appreciation, then quickly nodded.

"Suppose I do. I know spots ain't no one else has seen. You walk the streets enough you get to see things."

"Exactly," Margaret said, sitting down. "And would you by any chance know of a quiet, inconspicuous place to use as a"—she hesitated—"well, as a kind of hideout?"

"A hideout?" the little group whispered almost in unison.

"Someplace people could stay unobserved, and in case there was a little extra noise, nobody would hear." Margaret looked at her hopefully.

Rose squinted. "Like an abandoned, unused place?" she asked.

"That's it."

Rose thought for a minute. "Maybe," she said finally. "There's a couple of spots, but they need lookin' into. Could let you know tomorrow."

"Good." She turned to the others. "Now, here's your part. I'll need contributions of money and time. The more of you that help, the less the burden will be on the others. We'll need money for food, some household stuff . . ."

"Wait a minute," Durso interrupted. "Exactly what are we hiding?"

"Not what." Margaret chuckled. "Who. We're going to kidnap Mr. Zarchin, and we're going to hold him until he tells us where he put that coin." She smiled innocently at all of them.

The silence that followed was broken only by the thumping and splashing of the washing machines around them. No one spoke for a good fifteen seconds until Sid finally whispered, "Kidnap . . . that's illegal."

"So is murder," Margaret said curtly.

"But you just can't do that," Roosa broke in. His eyes

had thrown off any trace of the alcohol. "You just can't go and grab someone and keep them locked up." He sounded indignant, as though the idea were as revolutionary as a glass without liquor in it.

"Why not?" Margaret said flatly and leaned back in her chair with a cigarette. "Think of it. There are eight of us to look after only one person. Rose just has to find a safe place."

"But when the police find out, won't they know you're involved?" Rena Bernstein asked. She pulled nervously at a straggly wisp of hair falling out from under her woolen cap. "A man just doesn't disappear without causing a stir."

"What can they do?" Margaret asked. "Follow me? Don't you think I know how to shake off a tail?"

"Shake off a tail. . . . " Sid looked up amusedly. "If poor Oscar could only hear you now."

"Oscar," Margaret said with a sigh, "probably'd have a coronary. He never did understand there were times you had to stand and fight." She dropped her cigarette into an empty Coca-Cola can and waited until the hissing stopped. "And this is one of them. What do you say?" She looked slowly at each one. "Can I count on you?"

"But what makes you so sure he'll divulge the location of the coin?" Durso asked, gesturing with his pipe. "What's keeping him from outlasting us? After all, if he gives away the location of the coin, he'll be putting his neck in a noose."

"Not a very tight one," Margaret answered. "At least, not as far as he knows. Without the existence of a provenance linking the coin to Hannah, there's little chance he could even be indicted. He doesn't know we have it. Hannah didn't even know she still had it. No, if he is reluctant to tell us, it's because he doesn't want to lose the coin, the biggest prize in his collection. But think what he'd be losing every day in our charge. I found out he is very active in the financial markets, and of course he would be unable to transact any business. He will miss several coin auctions, one, in fact, that is coming up next week with a coin he is sure to want to purchase." She took a deep breath. "And on top of this, his living conditions with us will be rather spartan, a far cry from his normal life-style. Duck *à l'orange* will not be on the menu, nor will he be sleeping in silk pajamas. No, Joseph, I think he'll give in. I don't give Mr. Zarchin more than a week in our care.''

Pancher Reese, always the polite one, raised his hand slowly as though he were back in grade school.

''Still,'' he whispered slowly, ''how are we going to get him? Kidnapping ain't easy. If we have to use force, none of us is very big.''

''Big enough. Don't forget there are eight of us.'' Margaret looked around again. ''At least I think there are eight,'' she said pointedly. After some hurried consultation they all agreed. The only one who showed some hesitation was Bertie, and that was because she felt reluctant to help kidnap a man she'd had a chat with. But she went along, urged on by Margaret's unmoving stare.

''Good,'' Margaret summed up. ''Now all we need is a place to bring him, and once we have that we can go ahead with the plans for the actual . . . um . . . operation. Today is Monday. Let's all meet again Thursday morning on our bench.'' She looked around. ''I hope it's not raining then. I find this place a little stuffy.'' She smiled. ''Any questions?''

''How much?'' Rena asked all of a sudden. ''I mean how much is this going to cost us to hold him?''

Margaret stood up. ''I calculate three dollars and seventy-five cents a day. Split eight ways is forty-seven cents or three dollars and thirty cents a week. Mr. Zarchin will just have to learn how to live frugally . . . at least while he's with us.''

Nineteen

ROSE MOVED SLOWLY THROUGH THE SIDE streets that evening on her way to the places she had remembered. Her mission was considerably delayed by stops at a few of her favorite garbage cans along the way. The trash bin at Eighty-sixth Street and Broadway on the northeast corner, for instance, always yielded several fresh *New York Posts* which the returning businessmen left off on their way home from the subway. Then there was the private can outside Jimmy's TV Repair on West Eighty-first Street, which often had several half-used batteries and bunches of good strong electric wire for tying up bundles. As she walked, she muttered to herself softly. She cursed the corns on her feet and the misty weather and of course the awful pooper-scooper law, but in all that she never forgot what Margaret had sent her out to do. By ten P.M. she had visited all the sites and was back on Broadway starting on her usual evening telephone coin-return slots. After only twelve phones she found a dime and inserted it back into the top slot.

"Margaret, is that you?" she growled after the phone was answered. The voice on the other end of the line coughed once, then asked tentatively, "Rose?"

"I found a place, just like I told you I would."

"Where is it?" Margaret asked quickly.

"Seventy-seventh just off Broadway."

"Good. I'd like to see it tomorrow. I'll meet you at the corner at noon." There was a pause. "You think it's okay?"

Rose chuckled. "Wait till you see it," she said. "He could holler himself blue and still no one'd hear."

Margaret hung up the phone slowly. She looked at it for a second, then picked it up again and dialed a number.

"Bertie, Rose found someplace. If it's okay, we'll need some things . . . blankets, glasses, plates, that sort of stuff. I'll make a list, but I'll need you to help collect them. Where will you be in the afternoon, say around four o'clock?"

"At the Bliss Center," Bertie said without hesitation. "*Blithe Spirit* is on with Rex Harrison, and I wanted to watch it on their color set."

"Good. I'll be there at three thirty," Margaret replied. Now, she thought to herself, this better work.

Twenty

MARGARET HAD BEEN WAITING FOR TEN minutes the next morning at Seventy-seventh and Broadway when she finally spotted Rose trudging up. Her friend had two fewer bags than normal, and in her left hand she was holding a small flashlight. Margaret waved and made her way across to her.

"Mornin'," Rose said, very businesslike, and turned toward Amsterdam Avenue. Margaret trotted alongside. "First came to this place during the heat wave back in seventy-nine," Rose continued. "Coolest place around, and they still haven't fixed the lock." She snorted. "Dirtier, though. There it is." She pointed a few yards up the block, and Margaret stopped to look. Ahead was a low, dirty, unused, two-story building. It was so small that it appeared to be just two rooms, one above the other. The little building was wedged between an old restaurant on one side and a garage on the other side. The top floor of the building had a plate-glass window so covered with grime that it was just barely possible to see the cardboard boxes stacked up inside it. The first floor had only enough room for two doors, one of which was oversized. Between them was a strange antique mechanism that Margaret stared at for several seconds before she realized what it was. In front of the oversized freight door was a rusty gate. The smaller door was secured by a weathered padlock.

"Is it what I think it is?" Margaret asked with delight.

"An old meat locker," Rose answered. "Suppose it was for that restaurant, but they haven't used it in years."

Margaret walked over and touched the remnants of the old balance scale. It was rusty like the gate next to it and obviously hadn't been used in years. But she was still able to read the calibrations on its painted beam. To her right a car squealed out of the garage entrance and made her jump. Then she heard the squeak of the opening door next to her and turned in time to see Rose slip inside. She followed quickly. Once inside she felt as though a cold, rotten blanket had been dropped over her head. Until Rose flipped the little torch on, the only light came from the small cracks under the front doors. A cloying, acidic smell pinched at Margaret's nose and reminded her of stagnant water. The temperature drop, until she got used to it, made her shiver slightly. Then a thin beam of light shot out, and Rose handed her the flashlight.

"Here, look around."

The first thing Margaret noticed were the walls. They were wood and, if the front door was any indication, must have been about eight inches thick. A light-greenish mildew stain covered much of the surface and glistened in the reflected light. Margaret rotated the light in a circle and saw that the room was perhaps seventeen feet square. On the floor were two drains partially obstructed by discarded kitchen equipment. Cracked display cases sat alongside stained metal sink tops. Along one wall was a dingy staircase that led to the second floor. Beneath it was a single spigot that was probably used to hose down the floor.

"Quiet, ain't it?" Rose said, and for the first time Margaret realized that she was listening to her own breathing.

"Like a tomb," Margaret answered. "It must be the walls. What's upstairs?"

"Little office loaded with boxes. Toilet in one corner. Wanna see?"

Together the two women walked upstairs and opened the door. The room was light enough to see without using the flashlight. But the only things other than the stacks of boxes were two old chairs sitting next to a table. On the wall above the table were several pictures of naked women. A tiny enclosed corner of the room had the word TOILET hand-penciled on a dilapidated door. Margaret shook her head.

"Rose, it's perfect. We'll just need some rearranging. How safe is it?"

"Seen a trace of somebody else in here only once and that was Christmas seventy-nine. Can't imagine anybody'd start coming now." She shrugged. "Suppose you could always put a new lock on the inside. Outside one's a snap to jimmy."

"Well, I'll put it on the list for Bertie." She turned and walked back down the stairs. "Let's go outside. I want to look at the block again."

They left the little building after Rose signaled it was okay and walked slowly up the street. Directly across from the proposed hideout was an expanse of windowless wall that was the back side of a warehouse on the next block.

"That makes it easier," Margaret whispered. "No curious shopkeepers to watch us come and go."

Rose smiled. "Best thing's up ahead." After a few steps she nodded to the second floor of a loft building. Even before Margaret could look up, she heard a piercing scream that made her grab Rose's arm. Then she saw the sign: KARATE SCHOOL. TAE KWON DO, HAPKIDO, KUNG FU TAUGHT.

"Goes on all day and till late at night," Rose said.

"Screaming all the time. I figured between that and the garage and the wooden walls we could probably keep him there a coupla months."

Margaret clapped her hands together. "Rose, you're a genius. It's even better than I thought." She turned back to the little building. "Now show me again how you work the lock and then I'll go off to make my list for Bertie."

Arm in arm the two elderly women walked back down the side street, spent a few minutes in front of the building, then continued on to Broadway.

"See you Thursday morning," Margaret said to Rose in parting. "And thank you."

"Nothing 'specially hard about that," Rose said to herself as she walked away. "Not like she wanted to find a place with free heat. . . ."

Twenty-one

MARGARET SPENT ALL AFTERNOON ON THE list for Bertie. Besides the obvious things like blankets, plates, and eating utensils, she also included sponges and mops and disinfectant. A spartan existence was one thing, but she couldn't bear the thought of locking Zarchin up in the building in the condition it was presently in. She also included three dozen twelve-inch candles. She toyed with the idea of allowing a portable radio but concluded that it was best to keep the flow of information to a minimum. No radio, but she relented with the books. She pulled down from her own bookcase ten mystery stories, carefully tied them in a little bundle, and put them on her reading table in readiness.

There were also little odds and ends she wanted to include to make her friends more comfortable. A cushion for the chair, a little alarm clock, and extra socks for the nighttime. When she'd finished, she looked at the entire list, which ran to some forty-two items. "Bertie will need help," Margaret concluded.

The Florence Bliss Center was unusually quiet for a late Tuesday afternoon. Perhaps it was because someone had finally decided the front entrance foyer needed painting and the heavy fumes of cheap oil paint filled the entire premises. When Margaret arrived, she was surprised to see only Bertie and another woman camped out in front of the color TV. Bertie was deeply engrossed in the latest *TV Guide* and didn't see Margaret until she sat down next to her.

"Would you look at this," Bertie said, angrily glaring back down at the *TV Guide*. "Came all the way for *Blithe Spirit*, and it's not on eleven at all." She looked back up at Margaret with a scowl. "Where's station twenty-one? I never heard of that. My little set only goes to thirteen."

"UHF," Margaret said simply.

"And what's this HBO, WHT, and God knows what? That's where all the good movies are." She peered closer at the old color Zenith in front of her. "This one doesn't even have twenty-one either. What is this?"

The other woman got up and, without so much as a backward glance at Bertie, changed the stations. She adjusted the color quickly and backed up to her seat in time to see Reggie Jackson strike out. This was the final insult: tuning in a ball game when somewhere in the mysterious ether of airwaves shooting around them one could capture Rex Harrison. It was too much for Bertie. She abruptly tossed the *TV Guide* on the floor in front of her and got up.

"C'mon, Margaret. I could use some tea." She gave a last angry look at the TV screen and headed out the door.

When they were settled comfortably in the center's little

snack room, a hot cup of tea in front of each, Margaret brought out her list. With all the Formica and linoleum and fluorescent lights around them, Bertie had to squint when she looked at the piece of paper. The first thing she noticed was how many items there were. Before she had a chance to comment Margaret said, "Sid agreed to help."

"But, Margaret, where am I going to get some of this stuff . . . a tape recorder, for example. What's that for?"

Margaret took a sip of tea and leaned closer. "I think it will come in handy. Besides, the center here has one nobody uses. We can borrow it for a short time." Margaret coughed. "We just won't tell them till we return it."

Bertie raised her eyebrows in shock. "Margaret, are you suggesting—"

"I am."

Twenty-two

MARGARET WALKED AWAY FROM THE center with a satisfied feeling. Bertie was never hard to convince; she just needed some friendly persuasion. The arrangements were now made for their supplies. After a full day of cleaning by the whole group, they would be ready to move Thursday evening.

Margaret reached into her oversized handbag with its floppy handles and lifted out a cigarette. Lighting up in a breeze was always a problem for her, so she turned into a nearby doorway. She inhaled deeply after getting it lit and stepped out into the crowd of people returning home from work. It was five thirty.

A full block behind her another figure stopped and waited cautiously by a vegetable stand. He reached idly for a nearby orange and pretended to be studying it. As soon as Margaret stepped out and began walking again, he tossed it back and continued after her.

Margaret crossed to the little island in the middle of Broadway and looked to see if any of her friends were there. Eighty-seventh Street was north of her usual gathering place, so she was not surprised when she failed to recognize anyone. She looked at her watch and without hesitating continued on across Broadway and kept walking west. In two minutes she was in front of her favorite bookstore, Murder Ink. She couldn't think of a better way to spend a half hour before dinner than to browse amongst the thousands of mystery volumes in the tiny, atmospheric bookstore. This was the way bookstores used to be, she thought, like some cherished private library. There were no posters of movie stars and no bags with cats on them for sale. By one wall and facing toward the front window was a large oak desk behind which sat the proprietress. From where she sat she could point to any book on her shelves and tell you the title, author, and plot. In many cases she could even tell you the murder weapon. Margaret loved talking to her, especially about the new writers. This time, after a few minutes of friendly conversation, she leaned closer to the desk and asked for a serious recommendation.

"Something a little less obvious this time, dear," Margaret added with a frown. "I'm getting tired of guessing the conclusion before I've met all the characters." The proprietress, an attractive woman with dark hair, smiled. Her eyes scanned the shelves quickly and stopped about a foot from Margaret's head.

"*Trent's Last Case?*"

"Read it." Margaret shrugged. "Besides, I said something new, not from 1913."

"And did you guess it?"

Margaret chuckled. "No. To be honest, it's one of the few."

The smile spread wider across the proprietress's face and she stood up. "Me neither. Here." She walked over to the new-listings shelves and after a minute selected three titles and brought them back to her desk.

"It's just that very little nowadays compares with the old stuff." She sat back down and slowly gave a little description of each book. As she talked, she looked out the window as though she had to detach herself physically from all the other books in the store to concentrate better. She spent a great deal of time on the last book, even describing the author's previous works. When she was finished, Margaret picked each one up and studied their covers carefully.

"I think I'll take this one," Margaret said finally. "I'm not much for violence." She shook her head sadly. "Seems like whenever these new writers don't know where to go with a plot, they throw in a senseless murder. Usually with a corpse ground into hamburger meat. Quite unnecessary, really." She reached into her floppy handbag and withdrew some money.

"I'm sure you'll enjoy it," the proprietress said. She looked up. "By the way, why didn't you ask your friend to wait inside for you?"

Margaret was halfway to the door of the little shop before this last comment registered. She stopped, turned to the proprietress with a frown, and said, "Friend?"

"Yes, the guy with the red hair." The younger woman looked out the window for a second. 'Oh, he must have gone, but I could tell he was waiting for you. He was trying to look inconspicuous, but after you've read as many procedurals as I have you can spot that sort of behavior at a glance."

Margaret felt her legs go rubbery, and she reached out to the little desk for support. She slowly sank down into an empty chair next to her. A worried look came over the proprietress's face.

"Mrs. Binton, are you all right?" she asked. "You turned quite pale."

Margaret took a deep breath, rested for a moment, and then slowly stood up.

"It couldn't be," she whispered, shaking her head. She moved to the door and slowly turned the handle. But before she left, she looked back for a moment to the bookseller.

"Waiting for me—you're sure?"

"As though he were Archie Goodwin on a stakeout." The proprietress smiled. "Actually . . . no. Archie would not have been as obvious."

Margaret looked left and right as she cautiously left the shop but could see no one with red hair. She turned toward Broadway, but after taking a dozen steps she had no idea what to do. How could it be Zarchin, she wondered? I'm the fictitious Mrs. Sloan to him. No address, no point of contact. And yet, who else could it be? She took another few steps. Unless the owner of the bookstore was wrong. But, if it is Zarchin, I can't go home. She pulled up at the light on Broadway and waited through two changes while several possibilities raced through her head. Finally her eyes traveled to the street sign. It's eight blocks away, she thought. I'll have to try it. She pulled closer to her the handbag and the plastic bag she'd just gotten with the book, and without looking around she turned and headed downtown. At Eighty-second Street she stopped and wheeled around. Her eyes quickly searched the crowd of people on both sides of the avenue. She couldn't see Zarchin; but again a sixth sense told her not to go home. She turned left in the direction of Central Park.

There are only a handful of grand buildings located on the West Side of New York City. Margaret headed toward one of them, the Beresford, a twin-towered building so large it took up almost half a crosstown city block. The front façade faced the park and contained its main entrance. But the Beresford had several other equally busy entrances situated on Eighty-first Street, each with a doorman who carefully screened all visitors. These entrances were not connected by a central lobby. The only way to get from one bank of elevators to another was through the basement. This useless piece of information she had stored away three years earlier when Pancher was moonlighting as one of their late-night doormen. Margaret quickly glanced at the names of the doctors on the brass plaques by the Eighty-second Street maisonette entrances as she walked by. At Central Park West she turned downtown and approached the main entrance. As she walked through the door, a large man in his sixties wearing white gloves and a well-tailored uniform stepped over to meet her. His face was florid against the gray of the visored cap, and his voice held just a trace of County Cork.

"Can I help you?" he asked politely.

"Dr. Allen Geltzer," she replied without a moment's hesitation. She looked around the large foyer with bewilderment.

"Ah, that's to the right, madam, then it's the end of the corridor on your right." The doorman frowned curiously at her. His eyes wrinkled up in an expression of mild bewilderment.

"Excuse me, madam, you're sure it's Dr. Geltzer you'll be wantin', the obstetrician?"

Margaret felt her breath catch in her throat. She was sure her face turned almost as red as the doorman's.

"Yes, Geltzer." She edged away. "Oh, I see." She forced out a little laugh. "No, not for me. I've come to make an appointment for my daughter." She leaned closer. "Coming in from Chicago for the first time."

The doorman smiled broadly. "No offense?"

"Not at all," Margaret answered, beaming back. She turned and walked smoothly to her right. Now for the hard part, she thought. As she walked she pulled out some of the strands of hair in the tightly held bun at the back of her head. Then she rolled the sleeves up on her shirtwaist and, as a last touch, lit a cigarette and left it dangling out of one side of her mouth. She passed Dr. Geltzer's door and approached the farthest elevator thirty feet away mumbling to herself. She stepped in before the man on the car could stop her. After a second's hesitation she looked up and narrowed her eyes.

"Well, what's keeping you, sonny." she blurted. "Down to the basement. I've got a tub of laundry waiting on this detergent." She held up the plastic bag with the book inside. "The lady of the house'll be furious if I don't get back up in time to do the dustin'."

The young elevator man looked her over carefully.

"Did I take you down before?" he asked slowly.

"Must have been the other guy while you were on break. Come on, time's a wastin'."

Slowly he turned around and closed the doors. Margaret could feel the car descend. At the basement level he opened the doors again and Margaret had to make a quick decision. She faced a blank cement corridor. Fifty-fifty, she thought, and turned left.

"It's the other way," the elevator man said suspiciously.

"Of course it is," Margaret replied. "But I left the cart this way. Now, stop pestering and let me get back to work." The elevator man shrugged and closed the doors. Margaret heard the car rise again to the main floor. She turned and faced the basement of the Beresford, a veritable warren of interconnecting corridors, boiler rooms, storage bins, and dark empty spaces. She glanced at her watch. Ten minutes ought to be enough, she calculated, and went off in search of the laundry room. She found it next to a wall of electric meters. The room was empty and Margaret went over to a bench to sit down and wait. Within a few minutes another woman struggled in with a heaping basket of clothes. She sorted it into two machines, then turned and gave Margaret a curious look.

"Never seen you here before," she said. "You new?"

Margaret looked up with surprise.

"Today's my first day. Working for . . . um . . . Thompson in 12E."

"Pay good?"

"Enough," Margaret said, trying to avoid a conversation.

"What's good?"

"Four an hour."

"Humpfh," the other woman snorted. "What people will

try and get away with these days." She turned back to her machines and shook in some detergent. Margaret looked at her watch again.

"Course," the other woman continued. "I'm not saying four is bad as long as they make it steady. A day here, a day there. That's no way . . . too confusing."

Margaret crushed out the cigarette she had been smoking and got up to look for the wastebasket.

"I'm four days a week." The other woman beamed. "Kaplan, 4S." She plunged in the coin slide and added in a loud voice, "It's a pity, though."

Margaret sighed. "What is?"

"Headed for a divorce. I've seen it before. Signs are all there."

"That's too bad," Margaret said as she sat back down.

"Too few shirts he's got . . . always begins with the shirts. Getting them laundered elsewhere."

"Listen," Margaret said, getting up again. "Can you get to the Eighty-first Street side from here? I need another pack of cigarettes."

"Sure, second corridor on the left. Walk all the way down, then make a right past the bicycle room. Can't miss it." She watched closely as Margaret headed for the door. "Hey, if I'm not here when you come back, I'll see you."

"Next week," Margaret mumbled. Seven minutes had elapsed. She headed in the direction of the bicycle room, and by the time she found the elevator another two minutes had passed. Margaret pressed the bell and waited. Within seconds the door opened and she walked in.

"Main floor, please."

"Hot down there," was all the elevator man said and in no time deposited her in the marbled Eighty-first Street corridor. She walked toward the entrance and out the heavy iron door. Without looking behind her she turned west in the direction of her apartment five long blocks away. That should do it, she thought. In one, out the other. But she still couldn't imagine how he had found her. Perhaps it was just luck.

It was a few minutes to seven, and the light was quickly

fading. It was also that quiet time when people were either eating dinner or getting ready to go out. Few pedestrians were on the streets, and traffic moved with unusual ease. Margaret walked as quickly as her seventy-two-year-old legs would carry her. Occasionally she would turn around to check the street behind her. Not once did she see anyone who looked remotely like Zarchin. She crossed Broadway again without incident and suddenly realized how Zarchin had found her. Hannah must have mentioned while talking to him at Parke Bernet that she had just met a friend, a friend from the Florence Bliss Center. "Damn," she muttered. Why had she agreed to meet Bertie there? She stopped for the light on West End Avenue and stepped off the curb. So what. I'll just avoid the center for the next few days. She was still looking up at the light when she felt the pressure of the viselike hands on her waist. But it was the silence of Zarchin's stealthy approach that shocked her. She gave a little muffled cry and tried to turn around. But the grip on her waist kept her facing forward. All she could see was a blur of red hair and a twisted expression on Zarchin's face.

"I learned long ago," he snarled next to her, "never go where you're led." He bent closer. "Sorry you have to learn the hard way." His hands tightened even harder around her waist as forty yards away a panel truck sped to make the light. She was mostly hidden from where she stood next to a parked car. It would take a simple push at the right moment, and Margaret would become simply another accident statistic. No one was watching on the empty intersection. Zarchin could simply walk away unnoticed. His grip loosened just slightly in preparation for the push. The van was now only twenty-five feet away and well past the point where it could stop in time. Margaret didn't think; she reacted. She tried to brace herself by leaning backward and at the same time swiveled as much as she could to her left. As she started to feel the movement of Zarchin's arms outward, she gripped one of the handles of her leather bag as tightly as she could and thrust the other in the direction of the parked car. Everything then happened at once. She felt her feet lift off the ground and describe an arc as her body swung out. The heel of her left shoe caught the right-hand door handle of the van and snapped off. The arm holding the bag felt as though it were being pulled off. Then everything went wavy as she hit the pavement with a thud. The last thing she heard above the screech of the van's tires was running footsteps. Then she passed out.

Twenty-three

MARGARET OPENED HER EYES AND LOOKED into the roundest, whitest, most frightened face she'd ever seen. Her memory came back more slowly than her consciousness, so for a full five seconds she was confused as to why this strange man should be staring at her so intently. Moreover, he seemed to be bending over her! Then the pain in her arm started breaking through her haziness and in a flash she remembered everything. She tried to sit up, but the pain in her arm became unbearable and she gasped.

"You're hurt," the man said with concern as he helped her sit up. Then for the first time she realized she was still awkwardly gripping one of the long handles of her leather bag. She let the handle go and miraculously the bag still hung there. She traced the other handle up and saw that it was securely looped over the hood ornament of the Oldsmobile next to her.

"What kind of crazy thing you trying to do?" the man now said. "You almost wound up on my windshield."

Margaret, still a little shaken, could only think of saying, "I'm sorry."

"I see legs come flying out and then a bump. You sure you're okay? You shouldn't drink so much."

"Drink?" Margaret said with surprise. She followed his eyes downward. Two feet away was a nearly empty pint bottle of gin.

By now two other pedestrians had stopped to help, and they gently lifted Margaret to her feet.

"Need an ambulance?" one of them said.

"No, no, I'll be all right. It's probably just a sprain." She flexed her fingers and winced as a little knot of pain erupted in her elbow. "I think that's all." She took a few steps. "That and a new heel." She looked at the van driver. "Did you see anyone behind me?"

"I told you, lady, all I saw was your legs. Then I hit the brakes and skidded half a block."

Margaret turned to the Oldsmobile and retrieved her bag.

"I am sorry," she said. "Best to go home. Perhaps one of you would be kind enough to escort me. I think I'll lie down for a while. And maybe fix myself a stiff drink," she added. "A real one."

Twenty-four

A HAZY LIGHT FILLED MARGARET'S TINY bedroom when she woke up the next morning. The soft breeze that ruffled her curtains already had the hint of an unusually warm spring day. Margaret propped herself up in bed and fumbled for her matches. When she got her cigarette lit, she leaned back and eyed the telephone. Waiting now until Friday was out. Zarchin knew who she was and probably where she lived. They had to move and right away. Slowly she reached over to the phone and dialed Sid's number. After a minute the phone was picked up, and a sleepy voice answered.

"Sid," Margaret cut through. "Get everyone together. No, I know it was supposed to be arranged for tomorrow. It has to be today. I can't explain. On the benches . . . eleven thirty. Think you can do it?"

Sid grunted something into the phone, and Margaret smiled.

"Good, I'll count on you. You can start on the list with Bertie after we meet. I'll call her right away before she leaves."

"I think you can wait, Margaret," Sid said with a touch of irony in his voice.

"Wait? Why, what time is it?" Margaret again fumbled on the night table, this time for her watch.

"Oh, Sid, I'm sorry. I had no idea it was only six thirty."

"Six twenty-six," Sid corrected. "But who's counting?"

By eleven thirty the temperature had climbed to seventy-eight degrees, and getting a seat on one of the Broadway benches was as difficult as getting a whitefish at Zabar's Sunday morning. Margaret had no choice but to bring everyone to Riverside Park. They looked like escapees from a tour bus chattering away as they bunched up and bumped into each other on the two-block walk. When they had finally rearranged themselves and settled down, Rena Bernstein was the first to speak.

"Now tell us, Margaret, what happened to your arm?" She pointed to the makeshift sling around Margaret's neck.

"I think I've gotten Mr. Zarchin angry."

"Angry!" Sid leaned closer. "Margaret, I don't like this."

"Nor do I. That's why we have to hurry and get him under lock and key."

"But how? You still haven't told us," Pancher said.

"Everything has to be carefully worked out," Margaret said, "so we don't lose the element of surprise." She looked around. "Any suggestions?" There was silence for a second.

"If we only had more time," Durso said. "Then we could study his habits."

"But we don't," Sid shot back. "The only habit he has now is trying to knock off Margaret."

"That's right," Margaret said, smiling. "So that's what we'll use."

Seven voices shot out questions at once. Margaret held up a hand.

"I've been thinking about it all morning." She looked at Durso. "Joseph, tell me if you see any flaws in this. I call him up this evening at seven thirty and tell him I want to meet with him, but not in his house . . . somewhere else, somewhere safe like a restaurant. I offer a truce: no more attacks on me and I won't make any more calls on the police. I know it sounds terribly naive, but that's the way it should sound. I should appear vulnerable. I think he'll go for it. At least he'll go to meet with me."

"But, Margaret," Durso objected with a frown. "What if he has a gun?"

"We'll have to deal with that in the cab."

"Cab?" Roosa picked up his ears. "What cab?"

"The one he's going to hail at seven thirty-five after he gets off the phone with me."

Sid chuckled. "I see you've got this all figured out, Margaret . . . except for one thing. Where are we going to get a cabdriver to go along with a kidnapping?"

"Who said anything about a cabdriver?" Margaret looked at him. "Can't you drive?"

" 'Course I can drive," Sid said, "but I don't happen to have a cab."

Roosa smiled. "No, but I know where to get one, maybe for a half hour."

"Ah." Margaret beamed. "I thought so. I remembered

you used to drive a taxi several years ago. That's all we need, a half hour at the very most if all goes according to plan.''

Sid frowned and turned to Roosa. "Where can you get a cab for a half hour?''

"At Dubin's Cafeteria, the place where all the cabbies stop for dinner on the West Side. Cheap good food and plenty of hack stands nearby for parking.''

"And no doubt they leave their keys in the ignition while they're eating their burgers,'' Sid added sarcastically.

"I think I can take care of that,'' Margaret said. "At least Pedro's cousin can.''

"But what happens if the cab isn't back in half an hour?'' Rena Bernstein asked, shaking her tiny head. "Traffic or something, or the cabbie has a quick dinner? As soon as the driver finds his cab missing, he'll tell the police.''

Margaret chuckled. "Not if he's involved in pleasant dinner conversation about the old days.'' She looked straight at Roosa. "Think you could do it?''

He rubbed the stubble of his two-day beard. "A half hour, huh? Sure. Get an old timer, one that was around when Fifth Avenue was two ways, and I could probably bend his ear for an hour. Those guys are always looking for excuses to have a second cup of coffee. Gotta shave, though,'' he said somewhat self-consciously. "They don't like talking to no rummies.''

"Let's see,'' Margaret said. "That's Sid and Roosa. Joe and Pancher, I'll need you waiting a few blocks away. That leaves Rena, Rose, and Bertie. Rena, we need you as liaison at Dubin's. Soon as Sid spots a likely cabdriver and they start in on his cab, you give the word to Roosa inside. Then notify me when Sid's away. I don't want to call Zarchin before we're ready. Rose, you be the lookout at the hideout and give the high sign if it's all clear when the cab comes up. Bertie, you've got your list to do this afternoon, then you'd better stick with me. Try and get as much as possible by tonight. Sid, you, too. With luck we'll be all set by seven.'' She looked around at the eager faces. "Any questions?''

"Yeah," Sid said. "What if he wants to get out before Seventy-seventh Street?"

"Impossible," Margaret said. "Joe and Pancher won't let him."

Twenty-five

"MIND IF I JOIN YOU?" ROOSA ASKED casually, looking around the crowded cafeteria. He was balancing a sandwich and a cup of coffee on a small tray and leaning forward into the little booth. Before the older man with the coin changer on his hip could say anything, Roosa was sliding in opposite him.

"Always hard to find a seat around now," Roosa continued. "But they've got the best brisket in town, and they don't charge no extra for the onions."

The other man looked up and ran his eyes over his uninvited dinner companion. He grunted and went back to stabbing peas on his plate.

"Course it didn't used to be like this before the goddamn Belmore closed," Roosa added.

The other man looked up again, but this time there was a small light of appreciation in his eyes.

"You drive?" he asked.

"Used to . . . before it got to be a fuckin' hassle."

"Yeah." The taxi driver chuckled. "When was that?"

"Before Lindsay screwed things up and made New York 'Fun City.' When doormen threw on lights over their canopies so you didn't go blind looking for a fare after dark." He took a bite out of the sandwich and chewed it quickly. "And when the park was open all the time to take tourists on big-buck sightseeing trips." He shook his head. "I wouldn't get into one of those oversized sardine cans you guys drive now if you pried me in."

"Yeah, don't tell me, Mac," the taxi driver said. "It's a cryin' shame. You're right, I was there." He took a furious stab at a piece of carrot and looked back at Roosa. "Can't count on anything nowadays. I remember in the forties you'd look up the shipping schedules and meet the *Mary* or the other big ones when they docked. That was a guaranteed ten-spot to the Upper East Side with trunks and all. Now, you get a fare to Kennedy and you're lucky if you get back the same day."

"Goddamn gypsies," Roosa said, shaking his head. "Wasn't like that when I was behind the wheel. Hey, remember the Astor?" He smiled. "I once had this guy climb in the cab with a monkey. 'Astor Hotel,' he says. . . ."

Sid waited patiently with the motor running and his eye riveted to the front door of Zarchin's town house. Soon, he thought, if Rena called like she was supposed to. He leaned forward, still looking out the window, and switched on the radio. A slow forties melody came out and Sid adjusted the volume a little louder. Any minute now . . .

Margaret hung the phone up lightly and turned around. Bertie tried to read through the blank expression on her friend's face but was unsuccessful.

"Well?"

"I don't know." Margaret rubbed the side of her nose. "I think he'll go, but he sounded suspicious. I'm sure he didn't expect to get a phone call from someone he just tried to kill."

"Did he say he'd go?"

"No, he said he'd think about it. Then he hung up." She shrugged. "But we should get a move on. I'll get the doorman to help us with all this." She looked over the three cartons of paraphernalia on her living room floor. "We've got to get it to the hideout before they arrive."

"If they arrive."

"Have faith, Bertie. Mr. Zarchin's curiosity is going to get the best of him."

Jimmy Dorsey was running through the second chorus of "It's Only a Paper Moon" on the radio when Zarchin's front door suddenly opened. Sid tossed the butt he was smoking out the window, shifted to drive, and started slowly down the street. Fifty feet away he recognized Zarchin and instinctively pulled his cap even lower. When he had seen him the first time at Parke Bernet, Zarchin had been wearing a three-piece suit, but now he was wearing slacks and a brown suede belted jacket. The gold collar bar was still in place under a Paisley silk tie. As Sid pulled closer to him he faced forward and watched him out of the corner of his eye. "Come on," he breathed. "Come on. I know you need a cab." For an instant Zarchin stood on the street and seemed to be considering walking. Then at the last moment, just as Sid's cab pulled abreast of him, his hand shot out. Sid applied the brakes and angled over to the side.

"Sixty-eighth and Columbus," Zarchin snapped, and got in. At Broadway they turned south and drove at an even pace until the light stopped them at Seventy-second Street. Sid stole a glance in the mirror at Zarchin's face and felt a shiver run down the right side of his neck. Zarchin's eyes were set in a hardened stare at the driver's identification papers on the dash. His mouth was pulled into such a fine line that it might have been formed with a ruler and matte knife.

"Hey, Sprague," he said, sneering. "Didn't you forget something?"

Sid frowned for a second, then his hand shot out and fumbled with the flag on the meter. He had been concentrating so hard on the instructions that he'd forgotten to start the meter. "Sorry," he mumbled and pulled away as the light changed.

"I ever ride in your cab before? You look familiar."

Sid turned his head a little to the left, pretending to look out the side mirror.

"Could be. I've been driving twenty years."

"You ever pull a stunt like that again with me, I'll send your hack number to the commission." Zarchin leaned back into the seat. "Save it for the tourists."

Sixty-ninth Street flashed by, and Sid slowed and then made the turn on the next block. They came to a halt again at the light. Across the street on the far corner was the restaurant Margaret had chosen. Zarchin was reaching into his back pocket for his wallet when both side doors opened at once. Two men sandwiched Zarchin in between them.

"Hey," he said with surprise. "I'm not out yet."

"True," Durso said. "Don't worry, we'll let you know when it's time." Zarchin felt something hard and looked down at his thigh. The man who had just spoken was holding a pair of pliers open and pressed up against his leg. Zarchin made a motion for the door handle, but as the pliers started closing, his hand retreated.

"That's better," Pancher said on the other side. He withdrew from the frayed breast pocket of his old jacket the loveliest straight-edge razor Zarchin had ever seen. Pancher smiled. "Family heirloom," he said simply.

The light changed and Sid pulled away.

"Where are we going?" Zarchin asked.

"To your meeting. Only the location's changed," Durso said. He looked at his watch and spoke to Sid. "What kept you?"

"He only came out a minute ago."

"It's over a half an hour already. Suppose Roosa's still talking?"

"We'll find out soon enough," Pancher said as he gestured toward the police car just pulling up next to them. Both cars were stopped for the light on Seventy-third Street. Pancher kept the razor low, held against Zarchin's knee. Durso applied a light pressure to the ends of the pliers. Sid looked straight ahead and tried unsuccessfully to whistle "It's Only a Paper Moon." Zarchin turned his head toward the police car but otherwise sat still. This frozen scene lasted for a full thirty seconds while the policeman in the right-hand seat leisurely glanced their way. Just as leisurely he turned back, and the patrol car took off.

"Light's changed," Durso prodded, and Sid sighed heavily and stepped on the gas. In another minute they were outside the little hideout. Sid cut the lights and motor and they waited until they got the okay from Rose. Then very quickly Durso, Pancher, Rose, and Sid spirited their victim through the open door.

It was pitch black inside until the door closed behind them. Then slowly candles were lit in the corners of the room, and Zarchin's eyes became adjusted to the dim light. He saw six people staring at him, one of whom was sitting at a table with her arm in a sling.

"Here's one time, Mr. Zarchin, you did go where you were led," Margaret said. "Joseph, I think you'd better frisk him. Sid, you have the note?"

He nodded.

"Then take his coat and hurry back."

For the tenth time in the past two minutes Roosa looked anxiously at the door. After three cups of coffee and a continuing barrage of conversation, he was about to lose his dinner partner. The taxi driver's efforts earlier to make it back to his cab had been postponed by Roosa's well-timed anecdotes and even an offer of a shared piece of apple pie. But now he was wiping the last crumbs off his mouth with a napkin and already pushing his chair back. Still no sign from Rena and thirty-five minutes gone. Roosa got up, too, and together they walked toward the cashier. Roosa managed to arrive first. He handed over three dollars and fifty cents. There was a short wait while the cashier looked at him.

"Whatsamatter?" Roosa asked perplexed.

"Four dollars and forty-three cents. You owe me another ninety-three cents."

"Couldn't be," Roosa said. "All's I had is a sandwich and coffee."

"And pie."

"So what?"

"So, another ninety-three cents."

"You're kidding," Roosa exclaimed. He grabbed for the check. "Let me see that." He studied it for thirty seconds, leaning forward and blocking the cashier's booth. A little line of four people had formed behind him. Still he added, this time out loud, until he finally looked up.

"Never been that much before." He reached into his pocket and pulled out a handful of change. "Wait, I can do it exactly," he said, counting out nickels and dimes.

"Come on, buddy," the cab driver said behind him. "I gotta run."

"Sixty, sixty-five, seventy . . ."

"Step to one side," the cashier said impatiently.

"Seventy-five, eighty-five."

Rena walked in, stood by the front door, and nodded imperceptibly to Roosa. He quickly counted out the last of the ninety-three cents and stepped away. The taxi driver paid and left hurriedly. The first thing Roosa said to Rena was, "I need a drink. Forty minutes of nostalgia is a lot of work sober."

"Me, too," she answered. "Then we'll have a good laugh together."

"How's that?"

"Trying to imagine the look on his face when he finds his cab parked two cars away from where he left it."

"Make that a coupla drinks," Roosa said, and the two of them walked out and into the nearest bar.

Sid made it back to Zarchin's front door at the same time Rena and Roosa were taking their first swallows at Mc-Glinty's. But Sid couldn't join them yet. There was still another hour's work to do if everything was to run smoothly. He quickly slipped into Zarchin's expensive suede jacket and walked to the curb. Fortunately it took only three minutes for an empty cab to pick him up. He slid over behind the driver, and in a voice as gravelly as Zarchin's gave an address in Chinatown. He didn't say another word on their ride downtown. When they arrived on Mott Street, he paid and melted into the crowd of pedestrians on the street. A block later he walked into the Sun Yeh Wing Restaurant, hung his coat up quickly on the rack by the door, and went to the men's room. When he came out, he left the restaurant and took the subway north. They were on their third round at McGlinty's when he finally walked in. Rena looked up with a question written all over her face. Sid winked.

"Like clockwork," he said, put his foot on the rail, and ordered a double bourbon.

Twenty-six

"IT'S REALLY QUITE SIMPLE," MARGARET said. "You tell us where you hid the 1804 dollar, and we'll let you go." She looked benignly at Mr. Frenos Zarchin sitting opposite her in the other straight-back chair. His arms were tied behind him and, from the rope between his wrists, another rope descended under the seat of the chair and secured his shins to its two front legs. In the dim light Pancher had made sure of his work by tying twice as many knots as necessary.

"Lady," Zarchin said slowly, "whatever the hell your name is, if you have any serious intentions of holding me for another five minutes, I guarantee I'll have you and your gang of dried-up punks behind bars so fast you won't know what hit you—"

"Binton," she interrupted. "The name is Margaret Binton, and quite frankly I can't see how you're going to do that. Why, you can't even lift a receiver off the hook, and we don't even have a phone." She stood up and took a few steps closer to him. "Mr. Zarchin, this is not a game. We are not playing at cops and robbers here. We're deadly serious." She glanced quickly at the little stiletto that Durso had taken from Zarchin's side pocket. She looked back with a frown. "As deadly serious as you appeared to be. All your money and connections won't amount to a hill of beans until we decide to let you go." She took a breath. "Look around. The building you are in is absolutely sound-proof. The walls are close to a foot thick. This is a veritable fortress, Mr. Zarchin, and you will remain its sole prisoner until you give us the information we want." She pointed to one corner of the room. "As you can see, we are prepared for a little obstinacy on your part. That is two weeks' worth of provisions. There is water here and even a toilet upstairs. Everything you need for survival has been taken care of. The mattress I'll admit is thinner than usual and I do apologize for its unpleasant odor. I'm afraid it's the best we could do on such short notice." She turned and sat back down. She lit a cigarette with some difficulty with her one good arm and held the still burning match closer to Zarchin's face. The extra light now showed a glint of perspiration across his forehead. "I repeat, sir, we are not playing." She let the match drop into the ashtray on the table and watched as it spluttered out. For several seconds not another sound was heard. Zarchin looked furtively at the others in the room.

"You know this is kidnaping," he said finally. "And unless you plan to kill me, which I very much doubt, at some point you'll have to let me go." He threw his head back slightly. "What will you do then?"

Margaret inhaled deeply. "Oh, Mr. Zarchin, do not underestimate us. That would be fatal." She shook her head sadly. "When you're old and poor, friendship is the only luxury, often the only thing to go on living for. In your greed you destroyed friendships that went back dozens of years." She looked around. "We are in no hurry. We have little else to occupy our day. Each of us is prepared to keep you here indefinitely. If you assume otherwise, I am afraid you may not survive your ordeal.''

"We'll see.'' Zarchin snorted. "By tomorrow morning they'll be scouring the city for me. You think you can kidnap someone like Frenos Zarchin and get away with it?'' He leaned forward angrily and grimaced as the rope cut into his wrists.

"I do," Margaret said slowly. "Otherwise we wouldn't be sitting here having this conversation. Unfortunately, it's quite one-sided.'' She stood up. "I can see you are not yet ready to cooperate. We will talk again. In two, maybe three days' time. Perhaps by then you will see things differently.'' She walked to the door and motioned to Pancher and Durso. In the gloom the two men materialized like ghosts by her side.

"You remember what we agreed," she whispered. "Two people at all times, eight-hour shifts, and never untied. Three meals a day and water when he wants it. Bertie will fix tomorrow's food. If you have any questions, you can call me from the corner phone booth." She put a hand out and unlocked the inside bolt. "Sid and Roosa will be here tomorrow." She looked at Pancher. "You remember the code?"

Pancher grinned and put a hand on the doorframe. He rapped seven times with the opening beat of "When Irish Eyes Are Smiling."

"That's it," she said. "Keep your fingers crossed. I hope I sounded mean enough.''

"You had me convinced," Durso said and watched as Margaret smiled and silently slipped outside. Then the door closed, and they were left in the little hideout with the candles sputtering from the draft.

"Relax," Rose said to Zarchin. "This may take some time.''

Twenty-seven

THE PAPERS DIDN'T GET THE STORY FOR over three days. The first mention of it came in a small article in the *Daily News* buried at the bottom of one of the metropolitan pages. All it said was that a well-known businessman, Frenos Zarchin, had been missing from his home for several days. The police were asking anyone with information to please contact them. It ended with a description of Zarchin and of the clothes he was presumed to have been wearing the night he disappeared. Margaret read it over twice and smiled. Then she folded the paper in half and threw it into her wastebasket. She had taken the sling off the evening before and now had use of both arms.

I suppose it's time, she thought and struggled out of her easy chair. She'd been getting reports from Bertie every evening, but so far there had been no change in Zarchin's attitude. He refused to talk to any of them.

"Well, I promised three days," she mumbled, "and I can't go back on my word." She went to fetch her handbag and in another minute was down on the street.

It was a warm, clear day, and as Margaret walked south on Broadway for a moment she felt a little sorry for her captive. It was a fleeting thought, brought on more by the weather than by any twinge of contrition on her part. But the result of it was that Margaret stopped at her favorite fruit stand to buy something fresh for him.

"So." She tilted her head at Mrs. Lee, the sole proprietor of the little stand. "Give me your best orange."

"For you, Margaret," Mrs. Lee remarked with a smile, "it's always the best." She rummaged in the back of the mound of oranges and came up with one the size of a softball. She smelled it, squeezed it, and finally put it in the little brown bag. "I got nice melon today, too. You know how you like the Cranshaw." Mrs. Lee looked at Margaret expectantly.

"Not today, Suchi," Margaret said, taking the little parcel. "And how's Leo?"

Mrs. Lee chuckled good-naturedly as she always did at Margaret's mispronunciation of her six-year-old son Liu's name.

"The same . . . as wild as ever." She took Margaret's dollar and handed her the change. "Don't wait too long on the melon. All gone by Thursday."

Margaret nodded, promised she'd be back before then, and continued down Broadway to the little hideout.

The door opened cautiously after Margaret rapped the seven knocks. Durso shut it quickly behind her and breathed a sigh of relief.

"He's been shouting at us all morning. We had to put a sock in his mouth."

Margaret raised an inquisitive eye to Durso, frowned, then turned toward Zarchin. Even after three days of captivity he had been diligent in trying to keep up appearances. It was a standoff. His hair was wetted and neatly combed, his face closely shaved with Sid's battery razor, and his shirt still buttoned formally at the collar. The only incongruity in his image was the hundreds of wrinkles in his shirt that made him look as though he were wearing a used pillowcase. That, of course, and the sock in his mouth. Margaret walked over and pulled it out.

"Shout if you like," she said. "Then have this nice orange."

He nodded, picked up the orange, and said simply, "I'll need a knife."

Margaret clicked her tongue. "That would be most unwise. I think you'll find your fingernails will do quite adequately." She smiled and watched as he slowly chipped away at the peel.

"Is there anything I can do to make you more comfortable?"

Zarchin gave her a sardonic look.

"Short of calling my lawyer and a limousine, yeah, there is." He motioned to the ropes that tied his legs together, then wound around the chair and his waist. "You can loosen these ropes. Your friend here thinks he's tying tourniquets." He continued peeling the orange.

Margaret thought for a minute, then motioned to Durso.

"He's got to be able to walk. Tie something from one of his ankles to that pipe overhead." She pointed. "Make it just long enough to reach the table. Then tie something else from his other ankle that trails loose. If he tries to undo one of them just yank on the other one . . . hard. When he has to use the toilet, untie the one to the pipe and use the loose one like a leash. That way he won't get any funny ideas." She turned back to Zarchin. "While it is difficult for me to forget your efforts at helping me across that street, as your hostess I feel a certain obligation. Is there anything else?"

He shook his head. "No, I can't think of a single thing that's lacking." He finished the last fleck of peel and neatly halved the orange. "Would you care to join me?"

She shook her head.

"I can envision a lengthy stay here, Mrs. Binton. Certainly long enough to outlast you and your ridiculous friends. The pressure will be on you, not me. With each passing day the search for me will become more intense. You can't hope to last more than a week." He smiled and bit casually into one of the orange sections. "And as far as the 1804 dollar is concerned, you're crazy if you think you're going to get it out of me." A little drop of orange juice rolled off his lip and down his chin. He carefully dabbed at it with a napkin from the nearby table. "So, you see, the next move is yours."

Margaret got up and walked a few paces to where Rena was sitting by the little Sterno stove.

"Could we have some tea, dear?" Her friend nodded, and Margaret went back to the chair. There was enough light coming down the staircase and from under the two outside doors to require only one candle for additional illumination. The little stove lit with a pop, and Margaret turned back to Zarchin.

"Of course I understand your thinking. There is a certain preliminary period that must be gotten through to prove that we are serious. A week, maybe two, is necessary before you realize we are not bluffing. Also it will take that long for you to begin to lose hope that you will be discovered by outside means. Rest assured that I have not left that entirely to chance." She smiled at him. "The police will also go where they are led, and I will only call them when they are needed. After you tell us where the coin is." Rena brought over a hot cup of tea and Margaret thanked her. She blew on it carefully until she was able to take the tiniest sip. "It will all boil down to a gamble on your part, Mr. Zarchin. At some point you must decide whether you can 'beat the rap,' as they say on television. Even after giving us the coin—and I guarantee for our purposes it must be in the presence of the police (we are not trying to steal it for ourselves)—it is doubtful you can be convicted. You will probably hire the best lawyers in your defense, lawyers who might even have been able to get you an acquittal had you been seen plunging the knife into Hannah—which, unfortunately, you have not. You will want to speculate, if you haven't done so already, on whether a provenance exists to even link Hannah to the coin. You will no doubt try to remember if there is any way to trace the murder weapon to you. And in the background will be your counteraction of kidnaping and coercion against us which will confuse the legal issues as to the admissibility of evidence." Here Margaret paused for another sip. "You will have to consider all these things and satisfy yourself that giving us

the coin is not such a risk after all, because that, Mr. Zarchin, is the only way you're ever going to get out of here.''
She finished off the tea slowly and reached for a cigarette.
''As I said, I suspect this process will take a minimum of two weeks. In the end I am sure you will see it our way, if only because you are at heart a gambler. You gambled when you killed Hannah, and you gambled when you attempted to do the same to me. One more time to free you from this''—she looked around her—''experience is not too much to expect. That's my reasoning lest you foolishly think I am following any timetable. You are wrong, Mr. Zarchin. I believe the next move is yours.'' She got up again and stabbed her cigarette out. Zarchin's eyes followed her carefully as she brought the empty cup back to Rena.

''What if it's a standoff?'' He forced a smile.

''You'll never have another glass of Dom Perignon or a bite of trout amandine again. Think it over. I'll be back in another three days.'' She walked slowly to the door. ''Oh, yes, I almost forgot. The 1798 five-dollar gold small-eagle reverse went for one hundred ten thousand dollars at Stack's yesterday. I thought you'd be interested since it was one of the coins you mentioned you wanted.'' She smiled. ''Quite reasonable, in fact.'' She nodded, then turned and walked to the door. In another minute she was on the pavement and heading toward her favorite bench for an afternoon of sunshine.

Twenty-eight

THREE DAYS LATER MARGARET WAS IN-
terrupted at her breakfast by a knocking on her door. She put
the crossword puzzle down with a frown to listen. There was
a meeting scheduled that day with Zarchin, but at three P.M.
Certainly no one was supposed to meet earlier at her apartment. The knocking came again, and, tying her robe more
tightly about her, she rose and went to the door. With the
chain still secured, she opened it a crack and looked up into
the blue and smiling eyes of Sergeant Shaeffer.

"Open up—police," he joked. Margaret fumbled with the
lock while he waited patiently.

"David, what a pleasure." She motioned him to the table.
"There's some pound cake left, and it won't take a minute
for coffee."

"Thanks, but no," Shaeffer said. "I'm on duty. Morley
asked me to invite you over to the station house for a chat."

Margaret stopped cutting the slice of cake, put the knife
down, and looked up.

"What on earth for?"

"He didn't say, but I've seen friendlier expressions on
tow-truck victims." He reached down, finished cutting the
slice, and picked it up. "I'll wait."

Margaret gave Shaeffer an inquisitive look, went into her
tiny bedroom, and started putting on some clothes. After a
few minutes Shaeffer, well on his way through his second

piece of cake, called through the door. "What have you been up to?"

"Same old boring things," Margaret called back. "A little knitting, a little gossip."

Morley was standing with his back to the door looking out the window when Margaret and Shaeffer walked in. Margaret was carrying her handbag and another bag in which some yellow knitting yarn was spilling out the top. She put both bags down at her feet and took her favorite chair. Morley was polite enough, ostentatiously placing the Camels well within her reach. But after a few minutes it became apparent that he was holding himself in check. He was too preoccupied with little things, straightening a pile of papers, rearranging the pencils so they formed parallel lines across his desk. All the while he was talking about the legal responsibilities of the police department and about the problems created by unnecessary interference by members of the public. It was quite a performance and quite out of place, and Margaret recognized at once what was coming. Rather than suffer through five more minutes of his warmup monologue, she leaned forward and said, "Get to the point, Sam. I'm in the middle of a difficult sweater."

Morley flushed and slammed his hand down, upsetting all his good work with the pencils.

"The point is, what do you know about the Zarchin disappearance?" There was an ominous silence while Morley glared at her. "I don't believe in coincidences, and this one tops Nixon's eighteen-and-a-half-minute erasure. One week you're asking us to arrest some guy on suspicion of murder, and the next he disappears. What gives?"

Margaret leaned back again and fixed him with her most withering stare.

"Sam Morley. Are you accusing me of something? Because that's what it sounds like. Maybe you think I've got him drugged and stashed away under my bed. Humph." She pulled out one of Morley's cigarettes and lit it furiously. "I'll tell you what gives. From what I read in the papers, you've got a problem on your hands and a bunch of clues which lead you nowhere. Now you're clutching at straws. Not that I'm not pleased. Zarchin deserves whatever he gets.'' She inhaled and waited for Morley to speak.

"You mean you don't know anything about his disappearance?" Morley asked in an even voice. "I want to get this straight. You're up to doing a lot of crazy things, Margaret, but I don't think you'd lie to me."

She hesitated only a half second.

"Sam, I promise. If I know anything more about his disappearance than what I read in the papers, you can lock me up and throw away the key." She looked quickly at Shaeffer. "Honestly."

There was another silence while Shaeffer and Morley exchanged glances.

"What was in the note in the coat pocket?" Margaret finally asked.

"How did you know about that?" Morley demanded suspiciously.

"*New York Times* this morning. Small article in the back. If you want to check it, I saw the desk sergeant reading a copy on my way in."

"Goddammit!" Morley exploded. "Who gave that out, Shaeffer? That was not supposed to leak."

The young sergeant scratched his beard. "Could have been the bartender. He may have mentioned it to someone before we found him."

"What bartender?" Margaret asked, leaning forward. "The paper just said that you found Zarchin's jacket and it had a note in it."

"Christ!" Morley looked disgusted. He shifted his gaze a second to Shaeffer, then swept it back to Margaret. For several seconds he seemed to be deciding something. Finally he said, "What the hell. They got this far with it, they'll probably have the rest by tomorrow's edition."

He reached for his own cigarette, lit it in one angry motion, and leaned back in his chair. He blew out a cloud of smoke and peered through it. "You mention a word and it's the last time . . ."

Margaret sat back with a smile. "Go ahead, not even a syllable."

"Good." Morley dragged again on the cigarette and balanced it on the edge of the chipped ashtray. Margaret focused on the little coil of smoke as Morley began.

"The first thing we have is the statement of the housekeeper. She claims around seven thirty to seven forty-five while she was doing the dishes she heard the elevator descend and the front door close. It was not unusual for Zarchin to go out after dinner, so she paid it no attention. It was, however, usual for him to get back by ten the next day."

"Ten the next day?" Margaret leaned forward. "What on earth did he do all evening?"

Morley looked at her uncomfortably. Several seconds went by in silence. It was Shaeffer who finally answered the question.

"He had a friend he spent several nights a week with. A Mr. Winston Sands. A retired musician."

"Oh," Margaret said, leaning back slowly. "Well, of course these things happen. It's not surprising. Still and all, I don't think I would have guessed."

"Few have," Morley added. "Apparently he likes to keep it that way. Anyway, by eleven the next morning Honorée went up to his room to investigate. His bed hadn't been slept in but that was not unusual. So, Honorée, being a timid sort, waited. When he hadn't shown up by two o'clock she screwed up her courage, called up Sands, and asked if he was still there. We got a call from Sands five minutes later." Morley paused and looked at a little fly that had intruded into the conversation and was buzzing in circles over his head. As effortlessly as he had entered, the fly spiraled out through the open window, and Morley continued.

"So first we check out this guy Sands and he's clean as a whistle. Spent the entire night playing Brahms in some high school benefit in Connecticut. Got home by twelve thirty and the night doorman swears he came in alone and had no visitors all night. He's out. So we go to our standard MP procedure and check in with the hospitals, airports, morgue . . . things like that. Nothing. Then we get lucky. We find a taxi report of a single man being driven from directly outside Zarchin's address to somewhere in Chinatown. The time was seven fifty-five, but at that time of night there could be several minutes' delay for a cab. The cabbie was on duty, and we had to wait until the next morning to question him. Unfortunately the man had a lousy memory and couldn't describe the fare. He averages twenty-five a night and it was two nights ago. Except he thinks he remembers the guy's coat as being expensive, something like suede. We showed him a picture of Zarchin, but it didn't jar anything loose. So the only thing we got was a lead, someplace in the city to look. His sheet said he dropped him off on Mott Street." Morley took another puff on the cigarette. "The thing's already hit the papers, so I get an okay from Horgan to use a couple of extra men from the Fifth, that's the Chinatown precinct. By six that evening we locate the jacket. It was left on the coatrack at the Sun Yeh Wing Restaurant. Been hanging there for two days and has been something of a temptation for the bartender. He was going to give it another day and then liberate it. So we get a positive ID on the jacket from Honorée, not to mention the initials F.Z. on the lining."

"How did the jacket get there?" Margaret asked.

"Bartender can't remember!" Morley looked disgusted. "Too busy fixing drinks, he says."

"Too bad," Margaret said.

"Yeah. All we're left with is a jacket and a scrap of paper we found in the pocket." He leaned forward, opened his desk drawer, and withdrew a plastic envelope. He slipped his fingers in and withdrew a single crumpled piece of paper. Silently he passed it across the desk to Margaret.

" 'The two hundred thousand by Monday or else. Leo Lee.' " Margaret frowned. "Leo Lee?"

Morley sighed. "There's seventeen columns of Lees in the Manhattan directory. Not one Leo, and that's not including the Bronx, Queens, Staten Island, and Brooklyn. Seventeen columns, I checked. There's more Lees than there are Joneses.''

"The funny thing," Shaeffer interrupted, "is that his connections were with the New Jersey mobs, not the Chinatown ones.''

"Yeah, well, we're trying," Morley said. "We're asking our Chinese friends. The word is out on the street. We're just waiting. If there's a Leo Lee anywhere in New York, we'll get him.''

Margaret passed the note back and watched while Morley put it away.

"No fingerprints?''

"Are you kidding? Fingerprints are only for cheap novels," he said. "Last time I saw a clean print at the scene of the crime I was gonna frame it. No, we just gotta wait and hope something comes up. Zarchin was like an octopus. Looks like he stuck one of his legs in the wrong place.'' He crushed his cigarette out. "Then I thought of you.''

Margaret produced a lopsided smile. "I don't know if I should be flattered or angry. If you need advice, I'm afraid I can't help you. It seems to me like you've covered everything. If you want to know where I was on the night of Zarchin's disappearance, you'll have to believe in my honesty. I'm sure I don't have a satisfactory alibi.''

"Oh, I trust you, Margaret. No question there.'' Morley again fumbled with the pencils. "I just wanted to hear it from you.'' He looked up and smiled. "Our relationship has always been one of trust.''

"Absolutely," Margaret added.

"Also I did think perhaps you might have some suggestions.''

She shook her head slowly. "I'm afraid not.''

"No?" Morley looked at her closely. "Well, thanks anyway. It's always nice seeing you. Sorry for the inconvenience. . . .''

Margaret lifted her handbag off her lap and stood up. "Good luck," she said. "If I get any bright ideas, I'll let you know.'' She turned and waited while Shaeffer opened the office door for her. She stepped through and headed for the precinct exit. The door to Morley's office closed quickly behind her.

"I don't like it one goddamn bit," Morley snapped after a few seconds. "Something's off. She's hiding something."

"Maybe," Shaeffer said, walking over and looking out the window. He saw her shuffle by on the street. "Yeah, the coincidence of it bothers me, too. But who knows . . . he could have been heavily into the Chinese Mafia for cash and they caught him."

Morley shook his head. "I don't think he'd have trouble raising two hundred thousand. He could have covered that out of petty cash. It's something else." The two men were silent for a moment.

"I want you to put a tail on her," Morley said finally. "Something's still nagging at me."

Shaeffer raised an eyebrow. "A full three shifts?"

"No, two will do. Eight A.M. to midnight. I guarantee she's in bed by then."

"I can get the guys from the Fifth," Shaeffer said, but he had a frown on his face.

"What's the matter?"

"I never liked spying on a friend. We're supposed to be trusting her."

"Are you kidding? I wouldn't trust her to unwrap a stick of gum without getting into trouble."

"Okay, I'll see what I can do."

"By noon today!" Morley added.

Shaeffer turned back from the window and took a few steps toward the door. "I'll set it up right now."

"Ask Stanton to come in," Morley said. "Maybe he's got something on Leo Lee."

Shaeffer reached out, and at the moment he touched the knob a little knock was heard. Shaeffer pulled the door open and saw Margaret standing shyly in the doorframe.

"I am so sorry," she began as she walked a few steps into the room. "I almost got to Broadway before I remembered."

Morley looked at Shaeffer with guilt before he realized she couldn't have heard anything through the soundproofed door.

"Remembered what?"

"My sweater. David got me out in such a rush this morning I almost forgot I brought it." She reached down in front of Morley's desk and lifted the little canvas knitting bag with the yellow yarn spilling out. "For the janitor's son," she continued.

The two men looked at each other, and for an instant the frown crept back into Shaeffer's eyes. But then he shrugged and watched as she walked past him again.

"Keep in touch," she said on her way out.

"Oh, we will," Morley finished. "We will."

The benches were relatively empty so early in the morning, but Margaret wanted one all to herself. She had to walk up to Eighty-fourth Street before she eased herself down onto one facing south. Only a few pigeons were on the island with her. She let her handbag drop to the bench next to her and propped the little knitting bag on her lap. She sighed heavily and reached into the yarn. By now she knew where the buttons on the machine were located. She pushed one and waited a minute. Then she pushed another one and sat back. From inside the bag and muffled by the layers of yarn came Morley's gravelly voice.

"I don't like it one goddamn bit. Something's off. She's hiding something."

Twenty-nine

"WHERE HAVE YOU BEEN?" RENA BERN-
stein's voice was full of anxiety. "We've been waiting since
three this afternoon. We thought something happened."

"Something did," Margaret said. "Morley put a tail on
me. I could only get away at midnight and then I have to
sneak out the back way." She looked at her watch to check
the time. "Well, you might as well wake him up," she said.

"Oh, he's up," Sid said, uncoiling himself from the pillows in the corner. "When he's asleep this place sounds like
a sawmill." He yawned and stood up.

Margaret pulled a chair over next to the bed and sat down.
She saw that both ropes were still attached to his legs, one
rising to the pipe overhead, the other one trailing loosely for
a few yards along the floor. When she looked back to his
face, she saw he was now watching her.

"It's been six days," she began slowly, "and the police
are still as confused as when they began. They're looking for
a Mr. Lee, someone, it seems, who loaned you two hundred
thousand dollars and was so very anxious to be repaid that
he had you abducted from a restaurant in Chinatown." She
chuckled. "One should always repay one's debts, Mr. Zarchin." She reached into her handbag and brought out a copy
of the day's newspaper. "Here," she said, "in case I've forgotten something. You'll find it on page thirty-eight."

Zarchin hesitated for a few seconds, then snatched up the

111

paper. He held it to catch the light from the candles on the table and for a silent minute read the story. But rather than put it down at the end, he quickly turned to the financial pages.

"I thought you might be interested," Margaret said. "I took the liberty of removing the commodities and stock quotes. I didn't want to upset you unnecessarily."

Zarchin slammed the pages together. "Damn you!"

"However, I can tell you, if you're into copper futures," Margaret said, "you're taking a bath." Zarchin frowned. "A report came out three days ago showing record surpluses." She sighed. "Sorry. I suppose if you are in copper, a phone call would be worth several thousand dollars to you. Such a pity." She lit a cigarette and smoked it a third of the way down before Zarchin finally spoke.

"You came to talk about copper," he said sarcastically.

"No, I had hoped the conversation would get around to silver dollars."

"Sorry, you were wrong." He lay back and closed his eyes. A little smile played at the corners of his mouth. Margaret waited until she had finished the cigarette and crushed it out before continuing.

"You are being very stubborn, Mr. Zarchin, and in light of the Grimes auction, which takes place in just over a week, very stupid."

Zarchin shot her a menacing look. "How did you . . ."

"Everyone knows about the Grimes auction. Biggest private coin collection to be sold all year. I can't imagine you'd want to miss it." There was a silence. "Now do you want to talk silver dollars?"

Zarchin took three steady breaths, looked around the room, and said, "No, I want to talk about the food."

"Oh." Margaret was surprised. "The food. Is there something wrong?"

"Everything." Zarchin sat up and pointed at Rena. "That woman has the self-confidence of a worm. She can't even open a box of Ritz crackers without help, no less boil an egg. The one they call Bertie thinks noodles are a form of ballast, and that vegetables should be boiled soft enough to knot. And then on top of everything the lady with the bags keeps bringing me little treats from the streets like discarded Twinkies or chocolate-chip-cookie crumbs. The kind of food I'm getting I wouldn't serve to a dying animal. I can stand lumpy mattresses, dim lights, and foul air. I cannot stand a poorly made fettucini.'' He lay back again. ''What are you going to do about it?''

Margaret looked at Rena and Sid with a puzzled expression. Rena just shrugged.

''I don't know what he's talking about,'' Sid said, walking the few steps over. ''Bertie fixed a macaroni and cheese that smelled so good I even had some.''

''I rest my case,'' Zarchin said softly. He turned to Margaret. ''Look, do yourself a favor. A little saffron in the rice, caraway and fennel seed in the cabbage.'' He sighed. ''Ten dollars will cover it all. Maybe a little anise in the bouillon.'' He sat up again. ''Come on. I'm not talking truffles here.''

''I'm sorry,'' Margaret interrupted. ''We don't have ten dollars for nonessentials. We're cutting everything to the bone as it is.''

Zarchin slapped his forehead and shouted, ''I'll give you the goddamn ten dollars. Go to my housekeeper. She'll give it to you. Maybe she'll even throw in a packet of *champignons secs*.''

''I'm afraid that's impossible.''

Zarchin groaned. The room subsided into silence again as he closed his eyes in defeat.

''Silver dollars,'' Margaret said softly.

''Never.'' Zarchin rolled over. ''Go away.''

''As you wish.'' Margaret got up and walked to the front door. When she got there she motioned to Sid.

''I think it's working,'' she said in a lowered voice. ''You'll see, he won't last another week.''

Sid looked over his shoulder at the motionless form on the bed.

''Neither will we,'' he said and opened the door quietly for her exit.

Thirty

ZARCHIN FOUND THE NAIL THE MORNING after Margaret's visit. He noticed its thin head sticking an inch out from the wall at shoulder height in one of his slow tours around the little area. Pancher was on guard as well as Joe Durso, and they both watched him as he walked at the end of his ceiling tether. The other rope trailed behind him like a cut mooring. The nail he spotted had been lightly hammered into the wood to hold a paper or calendar. It was not very deep, and as Zarchin leaned casually against the wall, his thumb and index finger worked very slowly at dislodging it.

"Whatcha doing?" Pancher said.

"Thinking," Zarchin replied and moved on. In four minutes he was back leaning against the same spot. An hour later he had the nail out of the wall. Shortly afterward he lay down on the mattress, pulled the covers over him, and closed his eyes. Durso and Pancher went back to their game of gin. Neither of them noticed Zarchin's hands move under the covers toward the tip of his shoe. When he got up several minutes later, they watched idly as he again paced from wall to wall. If they had failed to notice him earlier acquire the nail, they also failed to notice him now drive it into the leather of his shoe each time his foot casually hit the wall. After ten minutes he sat down at the table. A little grin spread across his face. The nail was now solidly into the shoe with just an inch protruding. He looked down at the plain white bread and Fruit Loops, and the grin turned to a wince.

"Another hearty breakfast," he growled.

Sometime after lunch Zarchin started working at the rope on his left leg that connected him to the ceiling pipe. The loop around his ankle was just snug enough to keep his foot from slipping out, but the knot itself was so tight it felt like an iron casting. It was a big thing, the size of two lemons, and was comprised of five smaller knots. Sitting at the table holding a book in front of his face, Zarchin tried to work the end of the nail into the first of the smaller knots. He could barely see it between the table edge and his knees. The room was very quiet, so he was careful to move his foot without any noise. After several minutes of wiggling and turning his shoe, he felt the tiny head make a little opening and snake through. He leaned back in the chair and took a deep breath. Durso looked up from a magazine he as holding, glanced over at Zarchin, then went back to his reading. Pancher was by the far wall playing a not-too-honest game of solitaire on top of one of the discarded stainless cabinets. Neither sensed that anything was wrong. After another minute Zarchin started rotating the shoe with the nail in it in tiny circles, applying as much pressure as he could. In an hour he had enlarged the hole of the first knot to the size of a dime. In another twenty minutes there were only four knots left. He cradled his head in his arms on the table to smother the sounds of his hard breathing. After a half hour's rest he started again.

Thirty-one

AT MIDNIGHT THE LOBSTER SHIFT WAS DUE to arrive. Roosa was looking forward to the relief. For the past two hours he had been having a hard time in the airless room. Rose had dozed off earlier leaning against one of her stuffed bags, and he had decided not to wake her. Now as he sat in the dim light the only things that could keep him alert were thoughts of alcohol. At first he thought of different drinks he had never tried . . . a short list. Then he thought of favorite bartenders, different glass shapes, and the merits of hundred-over eighty-proof vodka. When the signal knock finally came, he was just trying to work out how many milliliters were in a magnum. He shuffled over, opened the door, then finally went to wake up Rose.

"Time to go," he said. "Bertie and Sid's here." He walked over to the new arrivals and pointed in the direction of the mattress. "He's been having a hard night, tossin' and turnin'. Didn't touch his dinner." He looked over at the uneaten Spam and peas. "Been quiet for only the last half hour."

"Nightmare?" Bertie said. "Seems to be breathing hard."

Roosa shrugged and bent over and picked up his cap from the floor. He helped Rose gather up her bags, and the two of them walked to the front door.

"He won't give you any trouble," Rose said in parting. "Read his book all afternoon. I think he likes it here."

"Let's hope not too much," Sid said and opened the door

116

to let them out. He watched for a few seconds as they walked toward Broadway. Then he closed the door, threw the bolt, and turned around to see Zarchin with a fork at Bertie's throat. The rope from the ceiling pipe hung loosely fifteen feet away. The other rope lay unconnected at the foot of the mattress.

"Over there!" Zarchin hissed. "If you don't want me to hurt her." Sid looked into Bertie's panic-stricken eyes, saw her face take on the complexion of unbaked dough, and walked over to the mattress.

"That rope," Zarchin indicated. "Throw it here."

Sid picked up the rope and walked slowly toward Zarchin. He was looking at his shoulders, wondering if he'd get a chance to level a punch.

"I said throw it," Zarchin yelled and dragged Bertie back.

Sid took another step and hesitated as Zarchin pressed the fork deeper into Bertie's neck. Then he tossed the rope lightly at the other man's feet. As Zarchin bent down to pick it up, Sid lumbered forward. He was still two steps away when he felt the stinging blow to his head as Zarchin cracked the rope into his face. He fell to the floor, dazed. Immediately Zarchin moved Bertie to a chair and tied her into it. Then he stooped and rapidly bound Sid's hands and feet. "Now," he said, "let's see how you like it this way around." Sid groaned as he tried to sit up. "I'd relax if I were you. You've got a good eight hours before your friends find you." He smiled maliciously, walked to the door, and slowly drew back the bolt.

Rose was almost two blocks away when she remembered Zarchin's uneaten Spam. She had intended putting it in her bag but forgot it when she dozed off. There was certainly enough there to feed her favorite tabby, the orange-and-white one that had made a home in an alley at Eighty-third Street. For the past month Rose had been putting food in the aluminum-foil pan the cat used as a dinner plate. The Spam would be a real treat, she thought, and stopped in her tracks.

"Whatsamatter?" Roosa said, stopping a few paces ahead.

"I forgot something," Rose said.

"Can't it wait till tomorrow?"

Rose shook her head, thinking of the last two nights when she had passed by empty-handed.

"Won't take but a minute. Go on." She turned and started back in the direction of the hideout. She was thinking of the soft sounds the cat would make and approached the door without the slightest caution. It was past midnight and there was nobody on the block. Suddenly she noticed the door to the hideout opening. "Now ain't that peculiar," she mumbled. She double-checked to make sure she was looking at the right door. When next she looked at the entrance, she saw Zarchin calmly backing out.

"What's this!" She felt a little shiver go down her back. As casually as could be, he turned to walk toward Broadway and saw Rose facing him only a few feet away. For a second neither of them moved. Zarchin's left ankle was red and swollen from all the chafing, and his face was even more haggard from the day-long effort. His eyes were already puffy and large from confinement in the dark room, and his red hair was ragged and dirty. His clothes were wrinkled and ripped and hung loosely from his body. He stood for another second deciding what to do; then he moved. In a furious limping charge, he rushed in Rose's direction, hoping to run by her or if necessary knock her over. But Rose saw him coming and had a moment to prepare. She raised her big stuffed bags in front of her and took a step to the right. She presented a formidable obstacle, and when Zarchin hit into her he seemed to bounce back like a rag doll. Rose glowered at him over the top of her bags.

"Oh, no, you ain't," she said, taking a step forward. He needed little encouragement. He turned quickly and ran the other way. She glanced at the closed door of the hideout and quickly made a decision. If she stopped to see about her friends, they'd certainly lose Zarchin. Without hesitation she hobbled after him.

Zarchin limped ahead on his swollen ankle while Rose, struggling with her six or seven bags in tow, tried to keep up. But Zarchin was outdistancing her. By Columbus Avenue he was already a half block ahead. It gave him time to try and flag down a taxi. Seeing the frantic and questionable condition he was in, two cruising cabbies passed him by without slowing down. Rose closed the distance to a few yards before he took off again.

The decision she had now was a painful one. If she kept all of her heavy bags with her, she knew she could never hope to catch up. If she left them behind, she was sure they would be stolen. She looked across the street and saw another empty cab pass Zarchin by, but this time more slowly. She gritted her teeth, took a quick inventory, dropped all but two of her favorite bags, and reluctantly started off again. Zarchin saw her coming and limped east down the side street.

The strange footrace continued, but it was still an uneven match. Even with fewer bags Rose could barely keep up and had to stop every so often to catch her breath. Zarchin was still pulling ahead, but now instead of futilely trying to hail a cab he was running from one phone booth to another along his route. He had no money, Rose realized, and was looking for a dime. He even tried unsuccessfully to panhandle a late-night pedestrian. With all that, he still maintained a block advantage over Rose. When he turned the corner on Central Park West, she lost sight of him for almost two minutes. She reached the avenue and frantically looked in the direction he had taken. She stood breathing heavily, but Zarchin was nowhere in sight. He had either headed back west on the next side street, or he had headed into the park. She picked up her two bags again and, half running, half walking, made it to the next cross street. She peered down the long crosstown block and frowned. Her eyes searched the trees, the stoops, the garbage cans. The street was full of places to hide. There was no movement anywhere. Then she spotted the unlit phone booth twenty yards away, and she caught her breath. He had found his dime. He was inside with his back to her talking animatedly into the receiver. Rose crept to within a few yards and set her bags down softly. He still hadn't turned around. The door to the tiny booth was closed and she couldn't quite make out what he was saying. But she knew

she had to do something fast. She looked down into one of
the bags at her feet and saw the discarded electric cord from
outside Jimmy's TV Repair. She pulled it out, doubled it to
make a slip knot, then moved to within five feet of the booth.
Zarchin turned and saw her at the same time she slipped the
wire through the handle. He reached out, but it was too late.
In little more than a second Rose had wrapped the wire tightly
around a metal flange on the outside of the booth. Zarchin
tugged at the door, but it would not open. He scowled at her
but continued talking into the phone. After another few seconds he finally hung up, turned, and put his full weight into
trying to pull open the door. But he was exhausted from his
escape and the copper wire was too strong. He fell against
the back wall of the booth and grabbed the phone to support
himself.

But if Rose had succeeded in trapping him, she had no
idea what to do next. The hideout and help were more than
six blocks away. They looked at each other through the glass,
Zarchin with an angry expression and Rose with a puzzled
frown. Zarchin rattled the door a few times, but it was only
to convince himself he was really locked inside. The night
wind rustled a tree nearby and the noise mixed with the
occasional hum of a car as it passed on the avenue twenty
yards away. Everything else was quiet. No one was coming
down the block.

"Who'd you call?" she asked in an anxious voice.

"Let me out of here, you old bag!"

"The cops?"

Zarchin raised his voice in a loud yell and the noise surprised Rose so much she took a few steps backward. The
phone booth muffled much of it, but it was still loud enough
to draw attention.

"Here, stop that," she said. Zarchin yelled again.

"Good Lord," Rose mumbled. She looked around and
her eye fell upon her bags a few feet away. She reached over
to the nearest one, remembering the candy tin and the tool
that was inside. Her fingers slipped down past layers of magazines, string, and plastic bags until they felt the lid; then

they wiggled inside and grabbed hold of a handle. When she straightened up, she was holding the ice pick she had found lying in the gutter after the May street fair. She walked back to the booth and, brandishing the weapon, told him to keep still.

But Zarchin eyed the ice pick and shouted even louder. She expected someone to run up at any moment, and as the noise continued she became more frantic. There was only one thing left to do to stop him. She quickly unwrapped the wire from the projecting flange, went to the door, and pushed. But Zarchin had seen her. Afraid now of being stabbed, he was keeping the door closed. Rose stepped back and took a breath. Zarchin eyed her silently.

"Open up," Rose said after quickly looking around her.

"You're crazy," he said, eyeing the ice pick.

"Open up. We gotta go back. I won't hurt you."

Zarchin shook his head and gasped out a no.

"Okay." Rose shrugged. "I'll have to get you." She pushed again on the door, this time with all her weight. The folding door buckled in the center and opened a few inches, but Zarchin had wedged his body behind the first fold and kept it from opening further. Rose kept leaning for a few seconds, but nothing happened. It was a stalemate. She relaxed, moved back a step, and looked around again. Still nobody. Where were the cops? When she looked, she saw Zarchin had the door closed all the way again and had a tired grin on his face. Then she realized all he had to do was outwait her and somebody would have to come along. Now there was nothing she could do to get him out. Then she noticed something and looked closer. There was a series of little louvers at the bottom of the booth for air to circulate. She studied them for a few seconds, then looked toward her bags. She remembered having put most of the matches in the Macy's bag, but that was now five blocks away. She cursed herself for having abandoned them.

"I knew I shouldn't a done it," she said angrily. Still she brought the two remaining bags closer and rummaged through them. After a minute she stopped, went back to wire the door closed just in case he tried to make a break, and then continued her search. Zarchin's eyes never left her. He looked on tiredly as she finished with one bag and moved on quickly to the other. Finally she found a thin book of matches at the bottom near a year-old *TV Guide*. She walked with them back to the side of the booth.

"You coming out?" she asked once more. Zarchin saw the ice pick still on the ground and shook his head. She took another quick look around her at the empty block, bent down, and lit the frayed edges of the magazine. Then she placed it directly under the louvers and stood up. The magazine didn't burn so much as smolder. It was damp from having been near the bottom of her bag and produced wispy white trails of smoke. Some of the smoke curled up the outside of the booth and disappeared into the night air. But a good part found its way in through the spaces and started filling up the tiny booth. Zarchin's smug grin turned to a frightened grimace. He moved back from the door and looked down at the openings where the smoke was coming from. He tried bending over to cover the openings, but the booth was too narrow. The smoke kept coming, and in another minute the air in the booth had a slight yellow tint to it. Zarchin started choking and coughing and one of his hands went to his throat. Even through the light haze Rose could see his eyes were turning red and tearing badly.

"Let me out of here," Zarchin gasped. "You'll kill me." He banged on the glass with his other hand, and Rose went to untie the wire. She figured her only chance was to try and bring him to the hideout by threatening with the ice pick. Except she ran into a problem. Somehow the wire had gotten into a knot around the flange, and her thick fingers could not undo it. She struggled unsuccessfully for a few seconds. Then she remembered the ice pick and started working away with that. Zarchin's pounding became more intermittent and finally stopped altogether. In another thirty seconds she had the knot untied and was able to open the door. When she did, a gust of the acrid smoke billowed out at her along with a limp body. Zarchin glanced off her and landed on the pavement. He didn't shudder or groan or make any sign that he was still alive. Rose cautiously turned him over and looked down into the tear-streaked pasty face. But now there was a bruise over one eye.

"Lord, I've killed him," she said. "What will I tell Margaret?" But she felt for a pulse and after a few seconds sensed the light beat. Then she looked closer and saw he was taking in the fresh air in short erratic breaths.

"Thank God," she muttered with a sigh. She hiked him up under the arms and dragged him under a stoop some fifteen feet away. She quickly went back for her bags and the wire and then set to work. In only three minutes she had his feet and hands tied together and connected by the wire to a pipe behind him. Then she propped him up with his head lolling on his chest and stepped back for a look. Needs one thing more, she thought, and in twenty seconds she had it. One of the garbage cans nearby yielded an empty bottle of bourbon which she laid by his side. There was nothing more she could do until she got help. Now, she thought, if only I can make it back before he recovers. She picked up her two bags and rushed toward the hideout.

Thirty-two

IT TOOK SOME TIME BEFORE MARGARET realized that the loud knocking she had been hearing for the last two minutes was not part of her dream. She opened her eyes slowly and turned to the little clock on her nightstand.

Something's wrong, she thought when she saw the time.

Something's definitely wrong. The knocking came again just as Margaret was putting on her robe.

"I'm coming," she called out and rushed to the door. When she opened it, Bertie was standing there with an anxious look on her face.

"What happened?" Margaret asked sharply. "You're supposed to be on duty. It's almost three A.M."

"Margaret, I had to see you . . ." Bertie looked behind her in the corridor, then stepped into the room. Margaret closed the door quickly.

"Well?"

"He escaped," Bertie said.

Margaret's eyes flickered slightly and her hand started involuntarily toward her heart. "He's gone?"

"He nearly killed me with a fork," Bertie stammered. "He was so quick I didn't know what happened. And he made a phone call. Rose told us."

"Rose?" Margaret looked puzzled. "Does Rose know where he went?"

Bertie's eyes opened as wide as poker chips. "But Margaret, he's back at the hideout."

Margaret shook her head in confusion. "He came back, on his own?"

"Oh, no, we brought him back. Rose, Sid, and I. And don't think it was easy."

Margaret took a deep breath and walked over to her favorite easy chair.

"Bertie, tell me what happened and from the beginning. Go slowly. It's very important."

"Of course, Margaret, I just hope we didn't do wrong bringing him back."

"Why?"

"Because of the phone call."

Margaret lit a cigarette she found on the table by the chair. "Okay," she said, "I'm listening."

It took Bertie almost ten minutes to bring her story up to the point where Rose, leading Sid and Bertie, came back to the stoop where she had left Zarchin.

"We approached very cautiously," Bertie continued. "Coulda been he came to and the cops were waiting. But we found him just like Rose left him, 'cept he was waking up and seemed a little woozy. Sid looked him over more carefully and said he'd be all right. He must have got the bruise over his eye when he fell out of the booth. We got him to his feet slowly and started walking him back. Let me tell you it was no fun." Bertie snorted. "He walked like he'd just had a quart of vodka . . . which of course gave Sid the idea."

"What idea?" Margaret asked.

"For the rest of us to act like we were drunk. Would have been too obvious without that. So there we go, the four of us, reeling down the street. When we pass anybody on the avenue Sid breaks out into 'When Irish Eyes Are Smiling,' and even if Zarchin wanted to say something they wouldn't a heard . . . or paid attention, for that matter. It took us forty-five minutes to get back to the hideout, and we were extra careful that no one should see us entering."

"And no police were waiting?"

Bertie fidgeted. "No, Margaret, but it made us nervous what with him making that phone call. Still, we didn't know where else to bring him."

Margaret thought for a minute. "No, you did the right thing. When he made the call he couldn't expect he'd be recaptured. Why mention where he'd been? I suspect he was phoning for help." Margaret closed her eyes for a few seconds and, except for her index finger, which was lightly rubbing the piping of the slipcover, remained motionless.

"It is very peculiar, though," she continued, "that in all that time the police never came." She looked at Bertie. "You did say it was about ten minutes after he made the call until Rose left him?"

Bertie nodded. "That's what Rose said."

"And another fifteen until you got back?"

"Uh huh. Of course the police could have come while she was fetching us, seen the booth empty, and figured it was a hoax."

Margaret nodded thoughtfully.

"Yes, or gone to the wrong location or even arrived after you left the second time." She stopped her rubbing. "Except I don't believe it. No, I don't think he called the police. Morley'd have someone there in under ten minutes, certainly under twenty-five." She sighed. "I think he made a mistake and placed his first phone call to someone he wanted to reassure. Just lucky for us. He had every reason at that moment to believe he'd escaped. In fact, under the circumstances I think it's quite natural. I probably would have done the same thing." She nodded slowly. "No, it wasn't the police. My guess is it was Honorée or even Mr. Sands. And that's why I think we needn't worry about bringing him back to Seventy-seventh Street."

"Good," Bertie said. "That makes me feel better. We all felt terribly guilty when he escaped."

Margaret smiled. "In fact, Bertie, if anything I think tonight's little episode has helped our cause. It may have shortened our waiting. Think of how numbing it must be for him. He's right back where he started. It may be the final straw. But now we must make sure he doesn't escape again. He won't make the same mistake twice."

"Sid has him so tied up he looks like a mummy. We're taking no chances."

"Good," Margaret said. "I'll let tonight's escapade sink in for a couple of days, then come to see him." Margaret smiled. "How's Rose?"

"Rose?" Bertie chuckled. "Rose couldn't be worse. Soon's we got Zarchin back and tied up she rushed out onto the streets again. Seems she lost four of her bags chasing him."

"That's a shame," Margaret said. "We'll have to make it up to her. She really saved the day."

"She sure did," Bertie said, getting up. "Without her we'd all be back on the benches of Broadway tomorrow twiddling our thumbs."

Margaret frowned. "Oh, no, dear, not at all. My guess is we'd all be in handcuffs right now."

Thirty-three

THE NEXT DAY DRAGGED BY FOR MAR-
garet. She went out to buy the different editions of the daily
papers and kept her radio tuned to the news station. But she
couldn't find any mention of new developments in the Zarchin case. By five P.M. it was obvious that whoever Zarchin
had called had not been in touch with either the police or the
press. But also no one had come snooping around the hideout. Their security was still intact and, as far as she could
tell, their plan was still running smoothly. She got this report
from Durso after his afternoon shift was over. He sat down
carelessly next to her on the bench, opened a magazine, and
spoke softly at the printed words in front of him.

"Zarchin is behaving a little peculiarly," he summarized.
"I thought you should know for when you see him next."

Margaret looked around, spotted the Chinese plain-clothes
policeman on a bench far enough away, and whispered.
"How peculiar?"

"He's angry, of course, and as sullen as always, but he's
definitely more nervous . . . almost like he's expecting
something to happen. He's not even complaining about the
food."

"Nervous?" Margaret whispered.

"Maybe it's just impatience, but somehow it's different."

"Mmm," Margaret mumbled. "I wonder, maybe he's
come to a decision." She stared back at the policeman a

127

block away for a few minutes without moving. Then she looked down and started rummaging around in her handbag.

"Joseph," she whispered. "I want you to do me a favor." She found the little scrap of paper she was looking for and opened it. "I don't imagine it will be too difficult. I'd like you to get information on a certain gentleman . . . a Mr. Winston Sands."

"Information? You mean where he lives?"

"No, I've already got that." She read out an address in the east Fifties. "I'd like to know his daily schedule."

"Not difficult!" Durso said sarcastically.

"Not for you, Joseph." Margaret closed her bag. "There are ways . . . doormen and things. You're always so gracious, I'm sure I can depend on you."

Durso was silent for a moment, then got up.

"When do you want the information?"

Margaret smiled. "Under the circumstances, I suppose it will have to be tomorrow. I'm seeing Zarchin in the evening. Ask Rena to take your shift."

"Under the circumstances," Durso replied with a grin, "I'll see what I can do."

Thirty-four

MORLEY PICKED THE PHONE UP ON THE second ring. He was still looking at the weekly overtime sheet when the unfamiliar voice interrupted his calculations.

"Evans here. Got a minute, Morley?"

"Who?"

"Evans. Nineteenth Precinct."

"Yeah." Morley squinted, trying to place the name.

"I got a little problem here, Morley. I think maybe you can help." There was just a trace of sarcasm in his voice. "I'm working on the Jansen murder . . . Parke Bernet knifing . . . remember?" He hesitated.

Morley dropped the time sheets on his desk and leaned back. "Yeah," he said slowly. "I remember."

"Problem is," Evans continued, "I got a loose thread that winds up on your side of the park." He took a breath. "In fact, right in your lap. My boys here figure we gotta check it so I said I'd call you direct."

Morley lit a cigarette. "What the hell are you talking about, Evans?"

"I'll walk you through it from the beginning," he said. "Two weeks ago an old widow named Jansen is murdered at Parke Bernet. We can't find a weapon, but the wound's a peculiar diamond shape and we figure it's got to be a stiletto or something. Into the picture comes a sweet little old lady who claims Jansen was her friend and was murdered for a coin." Evans paused for a second. "Name of Binton. Of course we've seen the type before and so have you. We get a lot of bored widows and pensioners as accident eyewitnesses and it's usually the same thing: stories so embroidered with fancy and speculation that they're picked apart by defense attorneys almost before they take their seat in the box. I figure it might be the same with Binton, but it gave us a motive, and I kept it in mind. Meanwhile I'm working on other angles, insurance policies to relatives, drugs, things like that."

"Get to the point," Morley growled. "You think I got all day?"

Evans chuckled. "So we tossed Jansen's apartment. We get a few slim leads on distant relatives, but nothing pans out. We interview all her friends at some old-age center to see if there are any grudges, but Jansen's got a rep like Mother Cabrini . . . everyone loves her. So where does that leave us?"

"With Binton's story," Morley supplied.

"Bingo. And so I go back to the apartment to see if I missed anything."

Morley crushed the cigarette out and leaned forward.

"And guess what," Evans continued. "I looked in the books."

"The books?" Morley said.

"Yes, each one. The first time around we just pulled a few and looked behind them. This time I turned the pages."

"Smart," Morley said in a tight voice.

"It paid off. We found two old brittle notes, each one said the same thing: 'Look in the Heine for the letter about the coin.' It was obvious that she'd forgotten over the years that she'd even stashed away the reminders."

"And the letter?" Morley asked, feeling the beginning of a pain in his stomach.

"Gone. The Heine was there. It had been recently opened. The dust had been disturbed, but no letter. It was easy to tell where it had been; the pages on either side showed a slight discoloration around the imprint. You following me so far?"

"Go on."

"Now, that leaves us only two possibilities as to who took it, Jansen or the murderer. I figure Jansen couldn't have taken it. She hadn't found any of the reminders, and if she knew to go directly to the Heine, she would have carried the letter with her to Sotheby's. The way she hid all those notes years ago it was obviously an important document. We had the lab double-check, and there's not the slightest trace of old brittle paper fiber in the bag or pockets of the clothes she wore when she was killed. She may have remembered she had an important letter, but it's clear she just forgot where she put it. But someone found it, and that had to be the murderer. Someone she may have told of its existence before she died . . . perhaps a friend." Evans let that sink in for a second. "We sealed off her apartment within three hours of her death, and at the time asked the standard questions of the doorman. He especially didn't recall the visit of a well-dressed middle-aged man with red hair . . . that was Binton's description. But after finding the notes three days ago I went back to the doorman and tried a long shot. I asked him if he remembered anyone that looked like Binton, and guess what . . . ?''

Morley held back the groan.

". . . He did, right down to the hatpin. That gave me a new angle. So I started piecing it together. First, she was there at Sotheby's and obviously had the opportunity. That means no alibi. Second, she had every possibility of finding out from Jansen of the existence of the letter and even of how valuable the coin was. Three, we've placed her at the murdered woman's apartment retrieving what was an essential document for her if she wanted to sell the coin. And four—and here's the killer, Morley—after asking around a lot, we've got a coin dealer, one Alexander Rosenblum, who swears that a Mrs. Binton—she even used her own name—came to see him regarding a rare 1804 dollar several days after the murder. It's pretty conclusive no matter how you look at it.''

Morley got up, and with the phone still to his ear he paced to the window. The twinge in his stomach had disappeared, leaving him with a hollow feeling, the type you get just before doing a backflip off a high diving board.

"So with that I did the only sensible thing. I put a tail on her just to see what I'd come up with. You know where she went? Boy, was I surprised.''

Morley went back to his chair and closed his eyes.

"She went to see you, Lieutenant Morley.'' There was silence on the line. "Now, perhaps you care to tell me why?''

After what seemed like a long time, Morley cleared his throat. "It's very simple,'' he said softly. "She's working for me.''

"Working for you?''

"That's right.'' Morley's voice rose. "And if you weren't such a goddamn East Side jerk-off artist and did your homework better you'd know that. She's in our community relations program, she's in here on the average of once a month, and right now''—Morley took a sharp breath—"she's helping on the Zarchin investigation.''

"Zarchin?''

"Yeah,'' Morley said defiantly.

"Well, buddy, all I can say is right now you got a murder suspect working for you."

Morley managed a laugh. "Who you kidding, Evans? You couldn't even convince a hanging judge with your story. Did you ever think that maybe there was a third note in the books which Jansen found? How about if she then put the brittle letter in a fresh envelope to carry around like a normal person might do? Also, if Margaret did take the letter, why didn't she show it to this guy Rosenblum, or even for that matter show him the coin? Then there's the doorman. This is my turf you're talking about, Evans. I know those West Side rent-controlled buildings like you know your fancy Fifth Avenue coops. I guarantee you, in any one day maybe thirty older women go in and out of them. That means maybe twenty-seven hatpins. Put that doorman in front of a lineup with Margaret and five other old ladies and he'll 'eenie meenie minie moe' his way till his eyes cross." Morley clenched his fist around the receiver. "Uh-unh, what you got might look good on a late-night rerun, but it won't cut it in a real-life court with a real-life defense, and if you don't know that, you shouldn't be sitting where you are." Morley looked up and saw Shaeffer had entered the room.

"So it's Margaret, is it?" Evans said slowly into the phone.

"Goddammit, I told you she comes in . . ."

"Now, listen to me, Morley," Evans interrupted. "As far as I'm concerned, she could be your goddamn mother. She's still a prime suspect in this half-ass murder. I might not have enough to pick her up now, but I'm working on it. I called because I thought that you might know something and by some incredible stretch of the imagination were sitting on it."

Morley shot Shaeffer a glance but didn't answer.

"I guess I was wrong."

"Listen," Morley said in a controlled voice. "I told you she's helping on this Zarchin thing."

"Well, I hope she's not essential because in a week she might have a new address . . . the Women's House of Detention."

"You're a real pal," Morley hissed. "Let me know when I can fuck up one of your investigations."

"I have my suspicions," Evans said, and Morley heard the line go dead.

"Shit!" He slammed the phone down and looked back at Shaeffer. For a few moments he didn't say anything.

"Son of a bitch! You know what happens if he finds out we're sitting on that letter?"

"Why didn't you tell him?"

Morley shook his head. "Too late. I should've told him right when she came with it. Now the only way to pull this off is to tie Zarchin in with it."

"Which is what Margaret wanted to do from the beginning."

"So where the fuck is he?" Morley said angrily and snapped a pencil in half. He looked down disgustedly at the broken ends, then threw both in the wastebasket.

"Easy," Shaeffer said. "Something will turn up."

"Yeah." Morley frowned. "Like my early retirement notice."

Thirty-five

ZARCHIN LOOKED AWFUL WHEN MARgaret walked into the hideout for her third meeting with him the next evening. He had not shaved since his escape attempt, and his eyes looked at her sullenly out of a drained and tired face. He watched intently as she sat down a few feet away and lit a cigarette. Even though it was after midnight, it didn't appear as though he had been sleeping. One of his hands was untied, and a book was open on his lap. Margaret returned his stare but didn't say anything right away.

"You know," she began finally, "it's really quite hopeless. I don't know why you persist." She waited but Zarchin remained silent. "What happened two nights ago was careless. I assure you it won't happen again."

Zarchin closed the book with a snap and narrowed his eyes.

"So you expect me to hang myself?"

"We've been through that already. I'm only asking for the coin. You get your freedom from us and all the legal help your money can buy. I think it's a fair gamble on both our parts."

"What if you have the provenance?"

"That's part of the gamble," she said evenly.

Zarchin leaned back against the wall and let the book slip onto the mattress.

"Mrs. Binton, you are a dangerous woman."

"Coming from you, Mr. Zarchin, I take that as a compliment." She crushed the cigarette out. "Now, let's get down to business. Lest you forget, Friday is the Grimes auction."

"Very dangerous," Zarchin reiterated. He closed his eyes. The only sound in the room was a slight hissing as a candle on the table sputtered in its little pool of wax.

"Also," Margaret continued, "you seem to have become stale news. Today's paper didn't have a single mention of you. I can't believe the police have been as delinquent as the press, but they don't seem to be any closer to solving your whereabouts." Margaret shrugged. "It's too bad you didn't phone them when you could."

Zarchin gave Margaret a black look.

"No, you are isolated, Mr. Zarchin, and the sooner you realize that, the sooner you can face reality. Your only hope is telling us where the coin is."

Zarchin leaned forward, and his tired face pulled into a challenging sneer.

"How do you expect to keep me honest once we leave here?"

"Oh, I don't think you'd want to do something foolish once we were outside. It would be most unfortunate. Our friend Pancher used to be a professional barber. He tells me that with a little flick of his knife, one you probably wouldn't feel, you'd be speechless. With another little flick, you'd be lifeless." She sighed. "Also there's Mr. Sands to think about."

Zarchin looked at Margaret as though he had been hit between the eyes with a two-by-four. He rocked back and took a deep breath.

"Winston?"

"That's right, Mr. Sands. I appreciate it's a private matter, and I see no reason why it shouldn't remain that way. No one has to know of your relationship." She smiled politely. "Mr. Sands will disappear just as quietly as Topper in the old movies. In effect he'd be taking over for you . . . doing your time. And don't think it wouldn't be easy." She unraveled a piece of paper from her pocket. "He is quite predictable. Rehearsals downtown at Twentieth and Sixth every morning at nine thirty. Lunch at La Gauloise at one. Afternoon walk in Central Park between two and four." She put the paper back. "During any one of those trips we could easily take him away as we did you."

"You wouldn't." Zarchin had raised his voice. "Winston couldn't take the confinement."

"That would be up to you." Margaret looked down at her feet. The candle that was sputtering finally went out and threw the room into deeper shadows. After a minute Zarchin whispered, "That's extortion."

"Yes." Margaret nodded. "I suppose it is. But in the family of crime I assure you it's a poor cousin to murder. So," she looked up, "what will it be?"

Zarchin looked at her with a queer little expression. Margaret could have sworn that just for a second she felt as though he were the captor and not the other way around. She remembered Durso's comment about his funny moods, his impatience. But then the moment passed and Zarchin said quite softly, "Just the coin?"

Margaret nodded. "Just the coin."

The tension in the room was so palpable that both Rose and Roosa, who were listening in their chairs a few feet away, reached silently for each other's hands. Zarchin's eyes glazed over and he lowered his head.

"Okay, just leave Winston out of it. Tomorrow morning. I'll take you there."

Margaret exhaled. "Where?"

He looked up with traces of anger. "It's enough you've won. You'll have to wait until then."

Margaret nodded. "I understand."

Zarchin's face relaxed. He looked at her for a full minute, then slowly leaned over on his side.

"I'll let you sleep," she said. "I hope your last night with us is a pleasant one." She got up and went to the door. "Shall we say nine, then?"

"No! Eleven," Zarchin answered brusquely.

Margaret frowned, then turned and left.

Thirty-six

MARGARET WOKE UP THE NEXT MORNING at seven thirty and dressed quickly. She would have preferred a nine o'clock appointment, for now she had two additional hours to worry. For example, why the delay in the first place? It seemed pointless. After fifteen minutes getting nowhere, she decided to divert herself with the crossword puzzle. After an additional twenty minutes she put the paper to one side and had a last sip of lukewarm tea.

"Eight fifteen," she noted with a sigh. "Now what?" She looked at her watch again to double-check, but the hands hadn't moved at all. Sid wasn't coming to take her to the hideout until ten thirty. Such a long time away, she thought, and decided to go out for some air. The room was stuffy, and just sitting there waiting made her anxious. She pocketed her keys and had reached for the door when she was startled by a knock. She stood for a minute, frowned, looked down at the way she was dressed, and finally called out, "Who is it?"

"Open up—police."

"Oh, David, you're always playing games." She unlocked the door and opened it to reveal the two stony faces of Lieutenant Evans and Sergeant Shaughnessy.

"I have a warrant to search your apartment," Evans said, and held up a sheet of paper. As he did so, Shaughnessy glided past her.

"A what?" Margaret said. She took a step backward in amazement.

"We have reason to believe you're hiding a certain document and a rare coin which are relevant to our investigation," Evans continued, stepping into the room. He turned and locked the door. "You will excuse us while we look for them."

"Wait a minute," Margaret said, but it was no use. Shaughnessy had already taken the pillows off the couch and was feeling deep down in the seams.

"What are you doing?" Margaret shouted.

"If you'll just sit down over there," Evans directed, pointing to a straight-back chair against the wall. "You'll be out of the way."

"I will not sit down over there," Margaret shouted back. "This is my apartment, you just can't barge in. . . ."

Evans rattled the paper again. "Yes, we can. Please sit down."

Margaret wheeled and watched as Shaughnessy finished

with the sofa and started in on the breakfront. "This is an outrage," Margaret said and reached for her umbrella. But before she could grab it, she felt a firm grip around her wrist, then a steady pressure leading her over to the chair.

"That will do. You're just making this more difficult for yourself." Evans released his grip and stood waiting. Slowly Margaret sank down into the chair.

"I was just on my way out," she said angrily.

"How convenient." Evans smiled, then leaned closer to the wall to look behind two of the hanging pictures. "I'm afraid you'll have to delay your outing. I wouldn't want you to accuse us of theft later on." He looked back at Margaret and his smile changed to a hard-eyed stare. "Or of planting evidence," he added, "especially to your friend Lieutenant Morley."

Margaret's face took on a look of incredulity.

"Surely you don't believe I had anything to do with Hannah's death?" she asked in amazement.

Evans started looking behind the pictures on the wall again and without turning back answered her.

"We wouldn't be here if we didn't think we'd find something."

Margaret was silent for a minute, then leaned back and looked at her watch. "Will this take long?" she interrupted. "I have an appointment."

"It's a good bet you'll have to cancel it," Evans shot back.

"I couldn't do that. It's terribly important."

"So is finding Jansen's murderer. Now, if I were you, I'd find something to read. The fewer interruptions, the quicker we'll go." Evans lifted the newspaper from the table and brought it over to her. "Here, why don't you try this."

"No, thank you. I'd prefer keeping my eyes on you. You're not going to find what you're looking for, and I want to make sure everything goes back in its proper place. For example"—she pointed to Shaughnessy—"that lovely pewter teapot belongs on the second shelf, not the third." Evans frowned, then motioned to Shaughnessy to correct the placement.

"All right," Margaret said. "Go ahead. And God help you if you break anything." She crossed her arms and watched them carefully.

Evans and Shaughnessy worked quickly. They were experienced and looked in hiding places Margaret had no idea existed: hollow curtain rods, telephone mouthpieces, between the layers of toilet paper. In two hours they had covered her living room, kitchen, bathroom, and were just finishing up on her bedroom. Both men's hands were covered with dirt from feeling in all the hard-to-get-at places. Evan's mood had long since changed, and he worked now with an angry expression. It was ten fifteen when he finally put down the last of the paperback books by Margaret's bed and called out dejectedly, "It's not here."

"Two hours of taxpayers' time wasted." Margaret snorted. "I told you that."

On his way past the desk Shaughnessy stopped and did a double-take.

"Wait a minute," he said slowly. "What's this?" He bent over and lifted a thin little knife from her pencil cup. It was Margaret's favorite letter opener, the one Oscar had given her on their honeymoon in Niagara Falls.

"Let me see that," Evans said. He walked quickly over to the desk. When he lifted the opener balanced on its two end points, Margaret felt a little chill run through her.

"Certainly you don't think"—she laughed uneasily—"that that knife was responsible . . ."

"I think," Evans said slowly inspecting the knife, "that it has an interesting shape. The laboratory will confirm if it's capable of making the wound that killed Jansen." He turned to the sergeant and in a lowered voice added, "Tell them to check it for microscopic traces of blood."

"The only microscopic traces you'll find will be little bits of Con Ed bills." Margaret waved her hand by them. "That knife's never been out of this apartment."

Evans turned on her. "You'll have to come with us to headquarters."

"Just a minute," Margaret said angrily, rising from her

chair. "I will not allow you to bully me. I understand all about my rights. There was nothing I could do against a bona fide search warrant, but if you want to take me down to your office I know there are only two ways you can do it, if I volunteer or if you book me. Habeas corpus and all that. You find it all the time in mystery books." She wagged a finger at Evans. "I'm not volunteering, so unless you're prepared to book me and take the consequences, I'm not going." She marched over to her favorite easy chair and sat down angrily. As she did she noticed the kitchen clock said ten twenty-five. God, she thought, it's getting late.

"Should I put the cuffs on her?" Shaughnessy asked and moved closer to her chair. He reached into his back pocket but the lieutenant raised a hand.

"Just a second." Evans sat down in the chair opposite Margaret. She noticed that even after two hours of hard work his tie was still neatly in place against his Adam's apple. Margaret raised her eyes and looked carefully at him.

"You know I could bring you down on 'probable cause,' " he said slowly.

"But it wouldn't be smart," Margaret said. "Not until you have the report on the knife." She shook her head slowly. "No, Lieutenant, the best thing"—she hesitated, looking for a particular word—"the tidy thing too do is to wait, and I think you know that."

There was silence in the room for a few seconds while Evans and Margaret looked unwaveringly at each other.

"Boy, she's a real talker," Shaughnessy said. "We gonna take her in?"

Evans coughed once and turned away. He took another quick look around the room and stood up.

"Put that knife in a plastic bag and let's get the hell out of here. I've had enough of this place." He walked quickly to the door, unlocked it, and waited for Shaughnessy to pass. Then he turned back to Margaret.

"I don't have to tell you to stay around. You couldn't go far or fast enough."

"I have no intentions of doing anything so foolish," Margaret assured him. "Only the guilty run."

Evans slammed the door shut behind him and stormed off down the corridor. Margaret exhaled heavily and glanced back at the kitchen clock. Ten forty! "Good old Sid." She laughed. "Thank God he's always on time."

Thirty-seven

WHEN MARGARET AND SID ARRIVED AT THE hideout a half hour later, they found everyone waiting. Margaret had decided earlier to keep the numbers to a minimum, and so only Sid and Pancher were going along with her to be the escorts. The others had been instructed to clean away all traces of their activities at the hideout and then disperse. But at a few minutes after eleven they were all there to congratulate each other on their success. Durso had brought a clean shirt for Zarchin to wear when he left, and after shaving, Zarchin looked a lot better. He still seemed pale, but the clean shirt and smooth face seemed to lift his spirits. Margaret gave him a brush for his hair, then undid the ropes around his legs.

"We won't need these anymore," she said.

Zarchin took a few shaky steps around the room.

"Can you make it?" Margaret asked with concern.

"Just get me out of here," he said quickly. "I'll show you how I can make it."

"Where are we going?"

"Grand Central." He stopped in front of Margaret and smiled.

"Are we taking a train, Mr. Zarchin?" she asked politely.

He chuckled maliciously but didn't answer.

"Probably a luggage locker," Pancher said under his breath.

"Okay, let's go," Margaret said. Sid and Pancher walked out with Zarchin between them. The door closed solidly, and the group of four turned west toward Broadway.

"Subway?" Sid asked.

"Too risky," Margaret said. She raised her hand for a taxi. In two minutes they were on their way downtown.

Fortunately they arrived at the terminal at eleven thirty, a good twenty minutes before the lunch-hour crowd would fill its restaurants and shops with masses of people. Even in the relative calm Sid still maintained his grip on Zarchin's belt, and Pancher walked close by on the left, his hand menacingly in his pocket. Margaret tagged along a few steps behind. So far their captive had made no attempt to escape or communicate with anybody.

Zarchin led them through the belly of the terminal. At each row of luggage lockers Pancher slowed his pace, only to find himself falling a step behind. They passed the ornate information booth and the ticket sellers behind their glassed-in enclosures, and still they kept walking. They walked down the long, wide corridor to Lexington Avenue until they came to the exit. Zarchin pushed through. Margaret rushed up and stopped the little group. People were passing by closely on the pavement.

"I thought you said Grand Central Station," she said with a frown.

Zarchin shook his head. "I said Grand Central." He pointed a half block north. "There's also a Grand Central post office." He looked at her smugly.

"Post office," she repeated slowly, and then a look of comprehension came to her. "Of course, postal boxes." She nodded. "Go ahead." The little group moved off again in the direction of the post office.

When they entered, Margaret saw a security guard wandering through the lines of customers answering questions. Zarchin also saw him but turned to his left. The lock boxes were on a wall near the guard, but Zarchin was heading to a large open window with a clerk behind it. Above the window a sign read BOXES 1-1221, 1581-3680.

"Just a minute," Margaret said and held him back. "Not yet." Sid and Pancher each grabbed one of his arms and waited. Margaret turned and walked back in the direction they had entered. She waited by the revolving glass doors until the Chinese plainclothes policeman who had been following her for the past several days ambled through. Margaret grabbed his arm lightly.

"Good morning," she said politely. "You really are doing a fine job." The policeman frowned and started to turn away, but Margaret's grip tightened. "No, you don't understand. I need you to witness something. I know you're from Morley." The policeman peered at her closely but didn't say anything. She tugged at his arm. "Come with me."

"Hey—" the policeman started but Margaret turned on him.

"Please, it's very important."

He hesitated for a second, then started following her. When they came up to the other three, she turned back to the policeman.

"Now, watch and listen carefully. You're going to have to repeat this in court." She nodded at Zarchin. "Okay, we're waiting."

Zarchin looked tiredly at the strange Chinese man's face, looked in the direction of Pancher's hidden hand, shrugged, and took a step toward the window. There was someone ahead of him in line, and while he waited he turned around and glowered at her. But Margaret did not return the look. Something had just occurred to her, and she was looking over to a clock nearby. Finally it was Zarchin's turn at the window.

"Box 2783," he said. The clerk glanced at him, apparently recognized the face, and went into a back area. In a minute he returned with a small stack of mail an inch high. Zarchin walked away from the window to a writing table nearby. Margaret and the policeman followed closely. Sid and Pancher were only a few feet away.

"How'd it get here?" Margaret asked.

"I mailed it to myself," Zarchin said matter-of-factly. "The afternoon after you left. This is a box I use for—special occasions."

"Yes, all your anonymous dealings," Margaret said.

A smile flashed across Zarchin's face and then just as quickly disappeared. He started sorting through the letters. His hands moved quickly, shielding any information on the envelopes. Finally he stopped, pulled out a letter, and looked at it more closely. Margaret saw a plain white envelope with a typed address and no return marking.

"This is it," he said. Quickly he opened the envelope by ripping it across the top with his finger. He inserted two fingers into the ragged opening, tugged, then ripped away another piece of envelope that was apparently obstructing the contents. The little scrap of paper floated to the ground as Zarchin withdrew an opaque glassine envelope. Pancher and Sid leaned closer to get a better look. Margaret narrowed her eyes, concentrating on Zarchin's hands. He reached into the glassine packet with three fingers, grabbed the coin, and flipped it back into his open palm.

"Here," he said, looking down at the coin. "The 1804 silver dollar."

"What this all about?" the policeman asked suddenly. "You call me over to watch some guy receive a dollar in the mail. You gotta be crazy."

"No, not any dollar," Margaret said, bending down. She found what she was looking for on the floor and straightened up. "And not just some guy. This is Frenos Zarchin," she said. "And I want you to arrest him for murder. That coin will prove it."

The policeman frowned, then looked from Margaret to Zarchin, then to Sid, and finally to Pancher. When he was finished a good twenty seconds later, he was thoroughly confused.

"Zarchin?"

"That's right," Margaret said. "And I want you to take charge of the coin and give it to Lieutenant Morley. It's material evidence."

"Hold it," he said, taking a step backward. "This is moving too fast."

"Then I suggest you call Lieutenant Morley. He'll straighten everything out. The number is—"

"I know the number," he said, raising his voice. "Now listen, no one move." He spotted a phone booth nearby and edged over.

"We'll wait right here for you," Margaret said. "We're not going anywhere." She turned back to her two friends. "Let's make sure Mr. Zarchin feels the same." She gestured with a nod of her head, and Sid and Pancher took up their positions on either side of their former hostage. Then she reached in her pocketbook and produced a dime. "I expect you'll be needing counsel," she said, and held out her hand to Zarchin.

Thirty-eight

THE ATMOSPHERE INSIDE MORLEY'S OFFICE was remarkably calm. It was obviously a tenuous respite at best. Everyone in the room looked ready to explode. To an outsider it must have been a strange sight. There was an old lady, two old codgers, a Chinese cop, a hippie, a well-dressed lawyer, and a middle-aged man with red hair and a bruised forehead. They were all standing, except for Margaret, who had conveniently grabbed the chair closest to Morley's desk. Zarchin's lawyer put his briefcase down and started to ask a question. The lieutenant held up a hand.

"Not yet," he said. "I want everyone seated and quiet." As they were looking around for seats, he picked up his cup of coffee and took a last disgruntled swallow. "Okay, what the hell's going on? Chan, why'd you bring this circus here?"

The Chinese policeman reddened and shifted in his chair. "Hey," he said, "I'm tailing her to get a lead on Zarchin, and she introduces me to the guy. Come on, what am I going to do, mail you a report?"

Morley scratched his chin and looked from Chan to Zarchin. "No," he said, "I guess not. Who are the others?"

"Friends of mine," Margaret piped up. "And witnesses, just in case Mr. Chan's memory is short." The plainclothes policeman gave her a nasty look, but Margaret was introducing her friends. "Pancher Reese and Sid Rossman. We were all together with Frenos Zarchin when he retrieved the coin he murdered Hannah Jansen for. That coin," Margaret added, pointing to the center of Morley's desk. There in a little clear space was the glassine envelope with the 1804 dollar inside. "On the basis of that coin and on everything else I've told you, I insist on your arresting him for murder." Margaret leaned forward and deftly plucked a cigarette from Morley's pack of Camels.

"Not so fast," Morley said. He looked at Zarchin's lawyer. "There's a lot at stake here. That's why I gave them fifteen minutes alone before I started. First of all, where the hell's he been for the last ten days?"

"Kidnaped," Zarchin burst out, pointing. "By that crazy old lady and the rest of her gang."

Morley looked over at Shaeffer and raised an eyebrow. The younger bearded sergeant folded his arms and leaned back in the chair as if to say, "Uh-unh, this is your show." He was having a hard time as it was keeping the smirk off his face.

"Kidnaped?" Morley said. He lit his own cigarette. "Mr. Zarchin, there've been no ransom notes, no demands. Usually in a kidnaping something is asked for."

"They were holding me hostage," Zarchin insisted.

"What for?"

Zarchin's lawyer put out his hand in time to attract his client's attention. Zarchin caught himself and shook his head.

"It's irrelevant," the lawyer said. "The fact is my client's been missing for close to two weeks whether or not any communication was received by the kidnapers. The offense is in the detention, not in any subsequent demands."

"But how do we know?" Morley said politely. "Maybe he just went on vacation. Maybe he took a powder for business reasons. It's been done hundreds of times before."

"Does he look like a man that's just been on vacation?" the attorney shouted.

"Sit down, Mr. Rusk," Morley said firmly. "This is not going to turn into a zoo." The lawyer straightened a flap of his jacket and sank down again into his seat.

"Chan, where'd the coin come from?" Morley asked.

"I told you, his post office box. Out of this letter." He leaned forward and dropped the white envelope with jagged edges on Morley's desk.

"Was he coerced?"

"Not that I could see," Chan said.

"What! That man has a razor in his pocket," Zarchin yelled. "They threatened to kill me."

"Check it," Morley said to Shaeffer. The young sergeant got up and moved next to Pancher and patted him down.

"He's clean," he said as he returned to his seat.

"It's absurd," Rusk interrupted again. "Frenos Zarchin is one of New York's most respected citizens, and you're showing doubt as to his veracity. He's being treated like a common criminal here."

"That's what he is, a murderer," Margaret said loudly. Once again the room erupted into a cacophony of curses and threats until Morley once again managed to restore order.

"One more of those and I'm throwing everyone in jail,"

he said angrily. He looked at Zarchin. "Is the box exclusively yours?"

Zarchin didn't say anything but looked over to Rusk for advice.

"Don't answer his questions," the attorney said. "You're not even under oath."

"That's right," Morley said, "but it would be easy for us to lean on the federal postal inspectors and have them subpoena the postal records to find out."

"But it doesn't matter," the lawyer said, raising his voice again and coming out of his chair. "Material residing in a postal box will not stand up as evidence of proprietary possession. You should know that. Anyone could have sent the coin to that box without my client's knowledge. You have to prove a prior connection."

"Yes," Morley said. "I do know that."

The lawyer looked at him with a puzzled frown. "And without that this is just grandstanding. There are easier ways to get your name in the papers, Morley. You arrest my client and you'll find yourself walking a beat in Canarsie . . . if you're lucky."

"Is that a threat, Mr. Rusk?" Morley narrowed his eyes and leaned forward. "I wouldn't want to see a man of your reputation lose your right to practice in this state because you got carried away and threatened an officer of the law in front of witnesses." Morley stabbed the cigarette out. Rusk looked around and, as though seeing for the first time the other people in the room, sat down quietly.

"Forget it," he said. "It just seems to me you're giving more credence to the stories of a bunch of misfits and derelicts than to someone of Mr. Zarchin's standing. My God, man, they kidnaped him."

"We don't know that for a fact yet," Morley said. He was about to add something when the phone rang. When he picked it up, Shaeffer noticed an immediate change come over him. He lit another cigarette and started playing nervously with the pencils on his desk.

"No, sir," he said. "He's all right. . . . No, I can't. . . .

It's not that simple. Yes, I know.'' Morley raised his voice.
"But it's more serious. There's a murder involved.'' There
was a long pause from Morley as he was obviously listening
to the caller. "Yes, I'll send it to you as soon as possible,''
he said finally. "I won't do anything until you look at it.''
He hung the phone up angrily and gave Zarchin a black look.
After a minute he said, "You can go.''

"What?'' Margaret squealed. "You're not arresting him?''

"No, I'm not arresting him,'' Morley said. "Not yet. The
DA wants a report.''

Zarchin smiled and stood up. Rusk collected his briefcase
and joined him.

"You haven't a case and you know it, Morley. When the
DA gets the facts, he'll press for a kidnaping indictment.
What have you got—a lousy coin that could have been sent
through the mails by anyone. As I understand it, you don't
even know it belonged to that old lady Jansen.''

"Oh, but we do,'' Margaret said and stood up to face
them. "We have the original provenance, don't we, Lieutenant.''

Morley looked pained. "Christ almighty!''

"But, Lieutenant, it's important that they know we're not
just woolgathering. We have the provenance.'' She pulled
back her shoulders. "We have my affidavit saying Zarchin
had the coin in his safe, and now we have the coin.'' She
smiled. "I don't know who the DA is, but when he gets those
facts, I think he'll see the light even though they were brought
to his attention by misfits and derelicts. In fact,'' she continued, smiling, "I think if he's smart he'll order another search
of your house, this time for a knife with a particular diamond-
shaped blade. I shouldn't think it would be too difficult to
find one in your collection.''

Zarchin's smile faded. "Bah!'' he said and whirled toward
the door.

"Just a minute,'' Morley said. "If I were you I'd stay
around. You're not under arrest; let's say you're under scru-
tiny.''

"What about them?'' Zarchin snapped.

"Same goes for them," Morley said. "Until this is cleared up you're all in hot water."

Zarchin turned and gave Margaret a last angry look, then walked through the door. Morley motioned to Chan.

"Write up a statement and leave it at the desk." The plain-clothes detective stood up and without a word followed Zarchin out. When Morley turned back, he saw Margaret deep in conversation with her friend Sid. He called Shaeffer over. "Make sure you got a man covering Zarchin's place. If he has the knife, I don't want him ditching it before we can get in again."

Shaeffer scratched his beard and lowered his voice.

"Sam, aren't you going out on a limb on this thing? You're playing it all out behind Margaret."

"I got to," Morley whispered angrily. "I'm sitting on that provenance. The only chance is tagging Zarchin with the murder."

Shaeffer grinned. "You think they really kidnaped him?"

"You're goddamn right I do. Leo Lee doesn't exist and never did. But if I let it play that way, how's it gonna look? Don't forget we conducted a search on Zarchin's apartment before he disappeared. No one's going to believe we didn't know about Margaret's zany plan and just turned our backs." He picked a pencil up again and bent it almost to the breaking point. "No, we got to make her charge stick. I'm banking on that coin. Let's hope it checks out."

"And if Zarchin brings charges?"

"Without evidence . . . he won't. There's not a jury in New York would find against a bunch of poor, law-abiding senior citizens like them. Besides, it's too crazy a story." He glanced over at Margaret, who was still talking to Sid.

Shaeffer straightened up. "Well, I'd better put Jacobson out. Think the DA will go for it?"

"Yeah, I think so. He's been after the guy for a while. But Christ, you never know."

Shaeffer took a last look at the coin in front of him. Then he turned and headed toward the door, almost bumping into Sid. Margaret was on her feet saying good-bye to Pancher.

"Just a minute," Morley said. He motioned to the two older men. "You can go, but I want a word with Margaret." Morley waited for the door to close. Margaret sat back down. A minute went by without anyone speaking. Finally Morley got up and walked slowly to the window. He looked idly at the rush-hour pedestrian traffic two floors below him.

"You know," he began, "there are about seven million people out there and maybe six and a half that hate their jobs." He turned around to face her. "I'm not one of them. I like what I do, good fringe benefits, good hours. I want to know why you persist in doing things to get me fired."

Margaret frowned. "I'm only trying to help bring a criminal to justice. Why should that jeopardize your job?"

Morley slammed a hand into the wall.

"By kidnaping someone!"

Margaret shrugged innocently. "There're just certain things the police can't do. There are . . . um . . . regulations you have to follow. I though I'd bypass them."

"Bypass them!" Morley exploded. "Margaret, you're crazy. I could throw you in jail right now on suspicion."

"What, an old lady like me?" She smiled. "Besides," she pointed out, "I got the coin, didn't I?" .

"The coin," he said slowly as he sat back down at his desk. Margaret had never seen him change moods so quickly. He pointed a finger at her and drew out his next words. "You got the coin, but you lied to me. You said you weren't involved."

"No, I never did," Margaret corrected him. "What I said was that if I'm involved, you could lock me up and throw away the key." She blushed slightly and looked down. "I have it on tape."

Morley glowered at her.

"Yes, I know, I was guilty of a certain lack of candor," she continued. "Turns out it was a mutual problem. However, I'm willing to take my medicine. If you want to lock me up, just give me a few minutes at home to get my toothbrush and things."

Morley leaned back and frowned. The honking of the horns from outside was the only noise in the room.

"This once, Margaret," he said finally. "I'll let you get away with it this once. You were lucky with the coin. But if you ever do anything again to jeopardize or compromise me . . . ever . . . I swear I will lock you up, if it's only in the basement of my house in Queens." He pulled his last cigarette and lit it, crumpling the empty pack.

Margaret got up, leaned over, and picked up the coin.

"But that's absurd, Samuel." She took the coin out of the envelope and held it up to look at. "Because I can't guarantee that I won't do something in the future that will displease you." She followed Morley's steps to the window. She sighed and looked out at the strings of people filing by. "But, Sam, we've known each other a long time, and our relationship is too good. I am ashamed to have allowed this distrust to creep in. I apologize. It won't happen again." She looked over her shoulder at him. "I hope you accept that, because now's the time to start afresh."

He looked at her closely and exhaled a thin stream of smoke. He felt faintly embarrassed. It was a moment before he spoke.

"I accept it, Margaret. I guess this whole mess is making me edgy. Yeah, you did get the coin." He stood and walked over to her. "I should have broader shoulders. After all, I've seen everything."

Margaret smiled. "No, Sam, not quite!" She leaned back as a look of confusion, then amazement, crossed Morley's face. But before he could stop her, she hurled the coin as far out the window as she could into the stream of pedestrians. They both watched transfixed as a small knot of people instantly converged at the spot where it fell. Then after some mild pushing and jostling, the small group quickly dispersed. The coin was gone, whisked away in the confusion of a New York rush hour. Margaret turned back from the window.

"As I said, Lieutenant, now is the time to start afresh."

Thirty-nine

HE HAD TO HURRY, SID THOUGHT. ZARchin had a ten-minute head start. What was it Margaret had told him he needed . . . chewing gum and yarn, but there was something else. He hurried down Broadway and walked into the well-lit A&P. It had been just five minutes since he'd left the precinct, but already he'd forgotten one vital item. Sid went immediately to the candy section and got a pack of Juicy Fruit, then headed for the home notions section. In his head he was trying frantically to remember what Margaret had said just before he left. Everything depended on it, and now he'd forgotten. He looked down at the small skein of blue knitting yarn and the pack of gum, and suddenly it popped back into his head. A can of sardines! That was it, sardines. He walked quickly to the canned goods section, found what he was looking for, and headed to the checkout counter.

After paying, he walked back out and turned south toward Zarchin's town house. The last time he'd tried something like what he was planning was over sixty years ago. He remembered that even then he wasn't very good at it. "If this works, I'll be amazed," he muttered as he waited for the light on Seventy-eighth. Fifty feet from Zarchin's door he stopped and pulled back into one of the doorways. Then he unwrapped two sticks of gum and put them in his mouth. It was five thirty, and there was a considerable amount of foot traffic on the block. But Sid could easily make out the policeman stationed outside. He was leaning against a car and looking not too subtly at Zarchin's front door. Sid took a few tentative chews on the gum and tasted the initial puckering sweetness. Then he felt the tenacious hold it developed on his dentures and cursed. "Christ, what I don't do for Margaret." Quickly he unraveled six feet of yarn and unwrapped the paper from the sardine can.

There seemed to be a lot of activity going on in Zarchin's house. Lights went on and off in different rooms, but most of the movement went on at the second floor. At one point Sid saw Zarchin come to the window and look out at the street, then quickly retreat from view. Very carefully Sid tied the yarn around the flat sardine can as though he were tying a gift, knotting it at the top center. Then he waited. The sun was sinking down behind the trees on Riverside Park, and a slight chill filled the air. Sid raised his collar and moved farther back into the doorway. Slowly it became dark on the street in front of him. The policeman was still there, but now he was sitting comfortably in a patrol car. His partner was at the wheel drinking a cup of coffee. Still no one had emerged from Zarchin's house, and Sid wondered if Margaret had guessed wrong. His jaw was getting tired of chewing such a big and tasteless wad, and he wished something would happen soon. He looked down impatiently at his watch and when he looked up again he saw Zarchin's basement door opening.

The policemen were talking and glancing only occasionally up the stoop. They missed the woman's hurried exit onto the street when a knot of people passed in front of the house. But Sid noticed and moved out down the opposite side of the street, keeping about thirty yards behind the woman.

The woman turned the corner at the avenue and headed south. She was still moving at a brisk pace and looking neither left nor right. Sid walked lazily behind her and let her get ahead. He didn't want to be too close. He stopped to tie his shoe, then continued on as slow and carefree as though he were out for a Sunday stroll. By the time she made it to the mailbox two blocks away, Sid was more than a block behind her.

In one smooth movement the woman reached into her handbag, pulled out a small envelope and, without looking around her, dropped it into the letterbox. Then just as quickly she turned and started walking back. She passed Sid at mid-block and didn't even give him a sideways glance. By the time Sid was nearing the mailbox, she was almost at Zarchin's corner. He waited until she passed out of sight, then reached into his pocket for the sardine can. At the same time he pulled the wad of gum into two halves and stuck each one onto the bottom of the can at opposite ends. Then he slowly approached the mailbox. He looked around once to make sure there was no one coming, then opened the slide and, holding on to the end of yarn, quickly put in the sardine can with the gum facing upward. As he closed the little metal door he saw the can slide downward and then he felt it flip over. When it dropped off the end, Sid slowly lowered his improvised snare into the box until he could feel no weight on the yarn and waited a second. Just then a car pulled to a stop at a red light five yards away and its driver glanced over at him. But Sid was hiding the end of the string balled in his hand and casually reached into his breast pocket as though he were looking for a letter. The light changed, and the car sped away. Sid slowly pulled back on the yarn until he felt the can catch on the inner lip of the slide. Then he gave it a quick little jerk and he heard the sound of metal landing on metal. He opened the slide wider, then pulled the can the rest of the way out. He saw stuck to its bottom two letters. The first was a bill someone was sending back to American Express. The other was a small envelope with a neatly typed postal box address in Scottsdale. Sid felt it and a little smile played across his face. He returned the American Express bill, pocketed the Arizona envelope and the sardine can, and kept walking. He hailed the next cab and gave the address of the Eighty-first Precinct.

Forty

FORTUNATELY THE HOLDING PENS AT THE Eighty-first Precinct were kept in a reasonable state of cleanliness. The floors were swept once a day whether or not there were any prisoners, and a fresh can of Airwick was placed every month on the barred window ledge. There was a bench along one wall, and, in case a prisoner had to be kept overnight, a cot with two very serviceable blankets alongside the other. It was on this cot that Margaret found herself at eight o'clock that evening talking quite contentedly with her only cellmate, Labelle. Labelle was a forty-year-old hooker who worked the strip around the Apthorp on Seventy-ninth Street. Her main crime this particular evening was to have moved her act a few blocks east to see what was happening at the trendy singles bars along Columbus Avenue. One of the bar owners had seen in the person of Labelle the seeds of reversing the Upper West Side revival and had called the cops. She sat now on the bench six feet away from Margaret and traded shopping stories. They had moved on to food, and to bakeries in particular, when the door opened, and Morley walked in. Labelle stopped in mid-sentence and gave him a casual look. Margaret turned around, inspected his face, and said anxiously, "Sid's returned?"

Morley's forehead creased. After a long five seconds he nodded once.

"I'll be right out," Margaret said. "Mrs. Belle was just

telling me about the Danish at Crawley's on a Hundred and third.''

''You'll do no such thing,'' Morley said angrily. ''You're staying in there until I say so.''

Margaret shook her head. ''Just a minute, Lieutenant. I have something to say in private, and either I go into your office or you discharge Mrs. Belle and we have this little cell to ourselves.'' She leaned forward toward her cellmate and lowered her voice. ''Please don't be offended, Mrs. Belle. It's just that there are some things that it's best not to burden others with.''

The younger woman smiled. ''Oh, no, honey, you go right ahead.'' She winked and sat back on her bench, smoothing out her leather miniskirt. ''I know just what you mean.''

Morley looked incredulously from one to the other, then after a minute pointed to Labelle.

''Out! She's not going anywhere, so it's you. Out. Go east of Broadway again and I'll throw you back in here for a week.''

''Not me, sugar,'' she said as she glided to the cell door. ''I'm going straight out and join the PTA.'' The door was buzzed open by one of the guards, and she stepped through. Then she turned and looked at Margaret behind the closing door.

''Thanks,'' she said and winked. ''You let me know if I can ever help you.''

''Don't mention it,'' Margaret said, watching her disappear through the doorway. Then she stood up and walked to the bars separating her from Morley.

''Well, what's keeping you?'' she said. ''Bring him in.''

Morley motioned to the guard again and the other man started for the door. ''And send Shaeffer in, too,'' he called after him. He turned back to Margaret. ''This better be good.''

''It'll be better if you give me a cigarette,'' Margaret replied. Morley felt reluctantly in his rumpled coat but only came up with a crushed empty packet. ''Sorry.''

Margaret shook her head. ''Don't you want one?''

"I'll wait."

"Thanks." Margaret glared at him. The door opened and Sid walked in with Shaeffer behind him. When the older man saw Margaret, he rushed over and touched her hand through the bars.

"What are you doing in there?"

She shrugged. "It's Lieutenant Morley's idea. He was upset over something I did. Don't worry, he'll get over it."

"Upset!" Morley bellowed. "Throwing away material evidence. Deciding on your own what is and what is not germane to a case." He shot the empty crushed cigarette packet into the corner of the room. "I'll say I was upset."

"But, Sam," Margaret said innocently, "if you'd used that coin you would have ruined everything. Now, just wait." She held out her hand in Sid's direction through the bars, and without hesitation her friend placed in it the envelope he'd just retrieved. Margaret pulled her hand back and opened the flap. Then she carefully shook out a smaller transparent plastic envelope, reached in, and with a finger on each side very slowly lifted out a silver coin.

"This," she said with a grin, "is the real 1804 dollar." She looked at it closely, turned it over, then replaced it in the plastic envelope. She nodded. "Thank heavens." She passed it through the bars to Morley. "Sid, you're terrific."

Her friend blushed. "But you told me what to do," he said.

"Just a minute," Morley interrupted. "You mean the coin you threw out the window was a fake?"

"Not fake, Lieutenant, what's known as an altered coin . . . probably an 1801." She smiled. "But a very good job," she added. "It nearly had me fooled. Zarchin was depending on its passing for Hannah's 1804 just long enough for us to enter it as evidence. Then he'd have sprung it on us. Of course that would have shot our case right out of the water. Those 1804 copies are a dime a dozen. Zarchin's a very clever man." Margaret nodded slowly. "It was the only strategy that was guaranteed to get us off his back and still not put him in any jeopardy. Very clever indeed. And I didn't figure it out until the very end.'' She smiled. ''That was one of the ingenious things about it. After he'd been held''—she paused—''shall we say, as our guest, for so long, I had absolutely no suspicions that he'd try to pass a phony coin off on us. I figured he had held on so long because the coin was real. He could have passed off a phony right after we captured him, maybe three days at most.''

''So, assuming this coin is the real one,'' Morley said grudgingly, ''How did you know the other one wasn't?''

Margaret didn't answer for a moment. She looked at Morley and then quietly asked, ''Sam, you're sure you don't want a cigarette?''

''Oh, Christ!'' He threw up his hands. ''You want a cigarette, I'll get you a cigarette.'' He stormed over to the door and stuck his head through. Margaret heard him shout someone's name. Morley came back with a fistful of cigarettes, lit one, and pushed it through the bars for her. ''Go ahead.''

Margaret inhaled peacefully on the cigarette, then continued her story.

''How did I know?'' she repeated. ''I suppose it was a bunch of things. Taken separately they were nothing more than curious, taken together they pointed unavoidably to the truth. First of all, I wasn't satisfied about the call.''

''The call?'' Morley said. ''What call?''

Margaret explained about Zarchin's escape attempt.

''I thought at first that he had phoned his friend Mr. Sands, but as time went by and Sands didn't notify anybody I had to abandon that theory. He certainly would have been in touch with you.''

Morley grunted.

''So that could have meant only one thing. The person Zarchin called was specifically told not to notify the police. It was very curious, but it was the only conclusion I could come to. But why not tell the police? How strange after being held for close to two weeks.'' Margaret turned away from the bars. ''Because he had asked the other person to do something for him and he didn't want the police to know. It was obvious you would question whoever notified you and that would be dangerous.'' Margaret sat down on the bench and puffed on the cigarette again. ''But the question still remained, what had Zarchin asked for?'' She looked at each of the three men standing in front of the cell before continuing. ''Next came the matter of the two-hour delay in going for the coin this morning. You'll recall, Sid, that after Zarchin agreed to lead us to the coin I said I would be by at nine A.M. But Zarchin was very firm; he would not go until after eleven. Of course that indicated something, but until I knew where we were going I had no idea what. Perhaps it was hidden in a museum that didn't open until mid-morning. But when he led us to the post office, which had been open since early morning, I knew something was funny. Why not go earlier, I asked myself. What happens at a post office between nine and eleven?''

''The mail is delivered,'' Sid broke in.

''That's right.'' Margaret smiled. ''The overnight mail is delivered to the boxes.'' She took another puff of the cigarette and crushed it out on the floor. ''Now, isn't that peculiar?'' she asked. ''How could Zarchin possibly know there would be something delivered to his box? He'd been with us all the time except for one lapse—''

''The call,'' Morley said. Carefully he lit his own cigarette.

''Yes, the call.'' She let that sink in for a minute while she rubbed the wool of the blanket next to her. ''But of course I had no proof. Nothing concrete. These were both surmises and could have been one hundred percent wrong. So when Zarchin brought his stack of mail to the table, I was very careful to watch closely. Because I knew for certain that there was a way to get my proof, and that was by the postmark on the coin's envelope.''

Morley frowned for an instant, then turned to Shaeffer.

''Get the envelope. It's on my desk.''

''That won't be necessary,'' Margaret said, and reached into a pocket of her dress. ''Because the postmark won't be there. Zarchin also knew it could be a giveaway, and so he very deftly opened the letter and by mistake ripped off a little piece. That little piece fell on the floor and no one saw." She opened her hand and in it was the small scrap of paper she had picked up earlier. "No one except me, that is. It was only because I was forewarned."

"And the date?" Morley asked.

"Two days ago." She got up and handed him the scrap. "Proof positive. Match up the ripped edges if you have any doubts."

Morley looked at it and squinted. "Still, all you knew was that he called someone and asked them to send a coin to his post box. It could have been someone he was protecting, an accomplice."

"Yeah," Shaeffer said. "It could have been the real coin."

"Not likely," Margaret said with a smile. "Zarchin knows so many dealers intimately he could have easily called one up and asked him to send an altered coin. As I said, they are fairly common and I'm sure Zarchin could have demanded silence on the dealer's part. But you're right, there was still a slim possibility of the coin's authenticity, which I could only have checked out after it was in our possession. By then, of course, it would have been too late. The real coin, the one you're holding, would have been in the mails and heading for the anonymous post office box in Arizona. But fortunately I didn't have to check it more closely. Zarchin himself gave the game away. After being so careful with everything, he made such a silly error. . . ." She shook her head. "I almost couldn't believe it."

"What did he do?" Sid asked wide eyed. "I didn't see anything."

"He touched the coin." Margaret chuckled. "He was in such a hurry to plant his false evidence that he dropped his guard for an instant. He put his fingers on the surface of the coin, and then he laid it in his palm."

"So?" Morley said.

"So." Margaret walked slowly to her right. "It had to be a fake. No expert would ever touch a valuable coin on its surfaces, especially a coin as rare as the 1804 dollar. Zarchin knew it was a fake and, as far he was concerned, it didn't matter. But it was as sure a giveaway as if I'd seen a blind man window-shopping." She stopped and turned back to them. "So then I knew. I saw what he'd done and realized that we'd been hoodwinked. But I also realized our only hope was to continue with the little charade. There was still a slight chance we might get the real coin and then his plan would backfire. We came back here and played it out. Then I waited until everyone but Sam had left, and got rid of the bogus coin. I had to, don't you see?"

"How the hell did you know you'd get the real coin?"

"I didn't," Margaret said simply. "I gambled that the coin was still somewhere in Zarchin's town house with the rest of his collection. If it was, I knew he would probably try to move it. The police were coming to search for the knife, and this time they wouldn't confine themselves to the obvious spots." She shot Shaeffer a meaningful look. "Also he knew by then we had the provenance. I made sure of that." She smiled. "The house was being watched; if he left, he'd be followed. The only thing to do was to send Honorée out. But where?" Margaret came back and stood in front of Morley. She touched the bars lightly. "Zarchin once told me that if something was worth doing once, it was worth duplicating. I figured that a man that had two wall safes and two security systems also might have two anonymous post office boxes. That was the only place where he would trust Honorée to go with the coin: a mailbox. It was simple, secure, and untraceable. From then on it was just a matter of telling Sid what to do. I must admit his execution was superb."

"First try," Sid beamed.

"Exactly." She looked back at Morley and grinned. "So now Mr. Zarchin is in for a big surprise. I'd love to see the look on his face when he finds out the coin he gave us turns out to be the real one."

Morley looked down at the coin in his hand, then over at Shaeffer. Shaeffer smiled. A little grin formed at the corner of Morley's mouth.

"Which leaves only one more thing," Margaret said. She tapped the crossbar in front of her nose. "My offer. As I said earlier, if you are planning on throwing away the key, I'll need a few things from home.''

For the first time in the past twenty minutes Morley noticed the bars in front of her. He looked at them with the same amused expression, then turned to Shaeffer.

"What do you think?"

"January," the young sergeant said with a chuckle. "Should be time enough."

"I was thinking of the spring," Morley answered. "Why put her out when she's liable to break a leg walking the slippery streets?"

"Hey," Sid yelled. "You can't do that."

"And think," Shaeffer added. "Home-baked cookies whenever we want them. Can set her up with a little oven and all the ingredients she needs."

Margaret was listening to them with a wry look.

"Okay," she said finally. "I can take anything but the sarcasm." She went and sat on the cot. "I'll stay."

Morley shook his head and went to the wall to press a button. There was a buzzing at the cell door again, and the lock sprang open.

"Come on, out." He jerked his thumb at the door. "It's open. Taxpayers got better things to spend their money on."

Margaret sighed and got up. "I am sorry, Sam. I guess I did put you through a lot. But we got Hannah's murderer, didn't we?"

Morley was about to answer when the desk sergeant stuck his head through the door.

"Excuse me, Lieutenant," he said. "There's some guy on the phone name of Evans from the Nineteenth. Says he's about to make an arrest on the Jansen murder and wants you to be the first to know. Sounds like a surly SOB." The desk sergeant looked around the room quickly, then back to Morley. "Want to take the call?"

Morley thought for a minute, then grinned.

"Tell him I'm busy." He winked at Shaeffer. "I'll let the DA break the news to him tomorrow after Evans has filled out his arrest warrant. Take him a year to live it down."

"You don't think he's referring to me?" Margaret asked wide eyed.

"Let's just say that if I were you I'd check into a hotel for the night," Morley said. He looked over at Sid. "Or some other anonymous location."

Margaret followed his eyes and frowned. "Why, Sam, I couldn't do that, it's not proper." Without hesitation she took a step and closed the door to the cell in front of her. "Besides, what could be more anonymous than here? I feel as though I owe you at least one night anyway." She went back and sat on the cot. She bent over, struggled for a moment, and finally removed her shoes. "The taxpayers be damned. Breakfast at seven thirty," she said when she straightened up. "Tea and English muffins will be fine. And, oh," she added, "don't forget the *Times*. I can't possibly start the day without the puzzle."

"Of course not," Morley said and looked at her with an impish grin. "Anything else?"

"Not that I can think of now," Margaret said. "But who knows, it's still early."

About the Author

RICHARD BARTH is a goldsmith and an assistant professor at the Fashion Institute of Technology. He lives in Manhattan with his wife and two children. *The Condo Kill* is the first book in the Margaret Binton mystery series.